FOOL ME TWICE

CARRIE AARONS

Do you want your **FREE** Carrie Aarons eBook?

All you have to do is **sign up for my newsletter**, and you'll immediately receive your free book!

PROLOGUE

S he had picked a light blue dress.

Normally, if you're being laid to rest, the family opts for black. Normally, the outfit would be reserved and bland, something that wouldn't draw attention to the fake color in your cheeks ... or be ruined as you were lowered into the earth.

But, I guess normally, one wouldn't actually pick out their own funeral attire at the age of eighteen. That was Catherine though, always wanting to be prepared. I remember the day she picked it, that she made me go online shopping from her hospital bed. It was morbid and made me want to vomit, but the first dress she pulled up was one meant to make me laugh.

The dress was skin-tight and leopard print, and wouldn't have covered her ass cheeks. It looked like something one of those reality TV skanks would wear at a jungle-themed party. It did the trick though, broke the ice as I began cackling into Catherine's bald skull. After that, I insisted on finding the perfect dress for her to wear when we said our final goodbye.

And dammit, we had found it. My best friend laid in her casket, two days over the age of eighteen. Someone, I think her mom, had picked the perfect shade of blond wig to memorialize her with. She'd lost all of her hair during chemo, but right now, as I looked at her, she looked like the old Catherine.

The one I met at dance class when we were four. The little girl I had my first sleepover with and was my first call when my parents finally caved and let me get a cell phone at the age of thirteen. Catherine was the one I cried to when my first boyfriend broke up with me, and I was there for her when her parents got divorced a year into her first recurrence.

She knew me better than anyone, and I her. And now she was gone.

I'm so goddamn mad, so heartbroken, that I could just about slap her right now. How dare she leave me? And how dare she pick a dress so beautiful, it only makes the jagged edges of my heart crack more.

The dress is the color of the ocean off some enchanted, exotic island. So blue and crystalline that it's almost translucent. It's more of a prom dress than something a person should be buried in, but I guess since Catherine didn't get to go to her prom, it's only fitting. The cap sleeves are made of lace, and the A-line skirt is laid right down to her simple gold flats that I know are under the casket lid, because I helped pick those out too.

If I pretend, it can almost be like she's Snow White, waiting for true love's kiss to wake her up. If only that was possible.

You think you're prepared for it ... the death of someone you love. But you can't know. You can't know the kind of dagger, the dull kind inserted slowly into the muscle that the world views as the symbol of love. It rips apart every piece of flesh, every nerve, every vessel, every synapse.

I thought I was prepared, I thought I could take the weight of Catherine's death, but as I stand here, looking at my best friend in the hours before I never see her face again,

I want to ruin something with my bare hands. Tear down the

world, scream at God. There is no reason for this, none at all. Who the hell decided a bright, gorgeous, hilarious teenage girl should be taken from the world at an age like this?

Who said I can survive without her?

I'm stalled, standing here in front of her too long. I can feel the eyes on me, the sympathetic ones, the reproachful ones, the pairs from my parents and Catherine's that are watching my every move, waiting for me to explode.

The list is in my pocket; I made sure to stuff it deep down into the lining of the beige pea coat that falls past my knees. Even though it's a cloudless May day and we're in the church, the one we made our first holy communions at together, I'm freezing. My bones are frigid, rattling together like they'll never get warm again.

My fingertip rubs against the worn paper. The ruler-sized notebook paper with three hole punches that Catherine ripped out of one of her school binders last year. She'd written the list in her scrawled cursive only a week after the doctor delivered the news that her cancer was back for a third time.

We knew then, what little time we might have. So my best friend wrote a bucket list:

1. ~~Go skinny dipping~~

2. ~~Travel to Paris~~

3. ~~Complete the local hot wing challenge~~

4. ~~Road trip to the ocean~~

5. ~~Send out a message in a bottle~~

6. Dye my hair

7. Have sex

8. Camp out in a tent

9. Go bungee jumping

10. Get revenge on Lincoln Kolb

We crossed off a bunch before Catherine got too sick, and the trip to Paris was done with her parents as one last goodbye trip. I think they knew that this time would be the last as well.

The night before she died, she called me into her hospice room and I laid down on the bed, pressing my cheek to hers. Without saying anything, she handed me the list. I knew what she wanted me to do.

So now, as I bend down to place one last final kiss on her forehead, I rub my fingers over the notebook paper.

This summer will be dedicated to crossing items six through nine off of Catherine's bucket list.

And when the first semester of my college career starts in August, so will the plan to take down the one guy who broke my best friend's heart.

1

LINCOLN

Three Months Later

"Fuck, it's a fantastic morning to be a fantastic stud."

I snicker at the statement as my sneakers pound across the pavement. My best friend, Janssen, isn't wrong, it's a fucking beautiful day. The perfect kind of scene for the first day of a college semester; bright, with sunshine streaming through every tree leaf and the smell of fresh-cut grass stinging our nostrils as we jog a brief five miles through campus.

Warchester University, the place I've dreamed of attending college since I could throw a damn spiral. They have the top football program in the state of North Carolina, division one, and last year they played in a championship bowl game. I've idolized the players who've run these paths, played in the stadium, and gone on to national league fame.

And now, it's my turn. Lincoln Kolb, national champion quarterback of the Warchester Bulldogs. Can't you just see it now?

"It is. But who said you're the stud?" Derrick asks, his breath coming out as if he's merely sitting on the couch.

I'm not out of shape by any means, but we're on mile four and I fucking hate running. It's why I'm a quarterback. I run short distances, and my arm is the one that makes me the big bucks. Well, not yet, I guess. And not that I care about the money. I'd throw a football for a living if you paid me in pizza, which isn't a bad deal now that I think about it.

But I've been working on my endurance this summer, gearing up to fight for my spot as QB number one. The senior currently occupying the position isn't declaring for the draft, and although he's won Warchester a bowl game, he's just okay. Me? I've been written about for years as the second coming of Peyton Manning. That job is mine, and I don't care who I have to defeat to get it.

"Chill, gentlemen, there can be two studs." I hold up my palm, glad that my fitness watch dings with a notification that our run is almost over.

"Meaning, not three?" Janssen pouts.

I shake my head, the bun I tied up at the top of my skull bouncing, our pace intensifying as we reach the last leg and hook a right onto the main path through campus. "Nah, you two can be the studs. I'm the big fucking man on campus."

My smile stretches across my entire face as I hold my biceps up in a flexing position, showing off as we encounter more students. I notice the way their eyes stick to me, both men and women, and I don't shy away from it. Being the center of attention has always been one of my favorite past times.

"You're a dick." Derrick smacks my arm, causing it to falter from its position in the gun show right now.

Janssen, who is one of the cornerbacks, runs to the right of me while Derrick, the starting tight end on the university team, runs to the left. We've been doing this run on weekday mornings for a month straight, ever since pre-season began, and now that the campus is filling up with other students, it's a bit harder.

Because ... *distractions, man.*

As we coast to a walk in the quad, I can't help but let my eyes linger over all of that exposed flesh. Freshman girls, upper-class girls, tan, skinny, curvy, short, tall ... all of these gorgeous co-eds sunning themselves and goddamn, it's a fantastic day to be a fantastic stud.

See, a lot of people view me as this cocky, arrogant asshole. Like I walk around with big dick energy and spit words that way too. I probably do. But if you'd seen half of what I have in my life, you would be the same way.

I don't take one day for granted. I don't leave any opportunity to be selfish, or take what I want, on the table. I don't hesitate to use a pickup line, ogle sexy girls, have another beer, go another round in bed, or to throw a fucking sweet Hail Mary pass.

You never know if you'll be breathing in the next second after this one. Which is why I take every chance those precious seconds give me.

"So, which group are we going to hook up with first?" Janssen rubs his hands together.

We've been living in the empty dorms for a month now, no girls in sight, and we're all horny bastards right about now. We've had our time to get the lay of the land, sneak our way into the best bars, and check out the coolest houses off campus. Now it's time to solidify ourselves. I wasn't joking about the big man on campus thing ... I'm fucking ready to own that title.

"Them," Derrick says before I can answer.

He nods his chin in a typical bro salute to the group of four blondes in tiny-ass bikinis. I groan as one flips over, the thong of her bottoms inching farther up those beautiful round cheeks. My cock twitches in my pants, and good lord these girls are smoking. God, I need to get laid. It's not healthy for a man to abstain for an entire month, much less an entire day.

But just as I'm about to head over there to chat them up, my phone vibrates in my pocket. Pulling it out as Janssen hands me a water bottle he must have gotten from someone, I unlock the screen.

It's a text from my dad, something about another hearing date. My smile falls as I read it, knowing that there is even more shit to come in the next couple of months.

My parents have been trying to adopt my cousins from my mother's sister for almost a year. Aunt Cheryl has never been the greatest mother in the world, but about two years ago she started dating her drug dealer boyfriend and the situation got too dangerous for the kids to stay. Now, the prick is trying to convince her to take them back, probably so he can use them or manipulate Cheryl more.

Tyla, my four-year-old cousin who loves Peppa Pig and unicorns, and Brant, an eight-year-old with the same penchant for football I had at that age, belong with us. Growing up, it was just my brother, Chase, and I. He's six years older than me, and lives in Chicago now, but we're still close. Our extended family was small, so when Tyla and Brant came along, it was like having more siblings in the mix. Except, they were younger and hung all over us and we freaking love them more than ourselves.

I would never put them in harm's way, and fire burns through my veins every time I think about what a shit parent my aunt is. Who would actively put their children in a dangerous situation? Who would pull them from a safe, loving home because of their own selfish reasons. It makes me want to spit nails.

But I can't worry about that now. The best way to show up for them is to play my hardest, study my hardest, and have a lot of fucking fun in between. Making it out of Warchester as the number one draft pick, and then signing a major rookie contract, is my number one goal. That's how I provide a better future for them. If this court case drags out, my parents will need the money, and I'll do whatever it takes to help them adopt my cousins.

"Bro, keep up. We need to invite at least half of the girls on this lawn to our party tomorrow night." Derrick raises an eyebrow to me like I'm stalling.

Shaking my head to clear the thoughts, I slap a big grin on my face. "Oh, hell yes."

I'll have a knockout practice today, solidify my spot as the game one starter, and then get hammered tomorrow night, and hopefully fall into bed with one of these hotties.

Goddamn, this year is going to be fucking awesome.

L ook at him, strutting through campus like he's got his dick in his hand, and every girl wants a taste.

Jesus Christ, he's preening more than a world-class peacock.

I pull my sunglasses down to the bridge of my nose, peering over them as Lincoln Kolb swaggers his way through the Warchester Campus quad. There are two other bros flanking him, big beefy guys who wear the same smug, shit-eating grins as their leader. How the guy is already a legend, by the way guys fist bump him and girls fawn as he walks by, escapes me.

It's like that scene in *Beauty and the Beast* when Gaston sweeps into town. All of his idiotic, adoring fans practically crawl on their knees in his wake.

Only this time, Lincoln Kolb may be their god, but I'm here to bring him crashing back down to earth.

Warchester University is the typical idyllic college setting. Perfectly green grass, massive oaks shading the exact right portion of brick and ivy-covered buildings. Benches, donated by each graduating class since the late eighteen eighties, lining the quad that is filled with students. It has its various clubs you can join, fraternities and sororities to pledge, and majors that vary from early childhood education to sports marketing. The weather is balmy for the end of summer in North Carolina, and there are more than a dozen girls in bikinis sunning themselves as Lincoln and his goonies leer over them.

Warchester wasn't my first choice. Wasn't even my second. I had my sights set on a liberal arts college in the middle of New York City. It has a kick-ass photography program, and the city provides the perfect canvas for the type of street, close subject photography I like to shoot. I even got in, back before Catherine died and my whole life changed.

But this was my promise to her. And to fulfill every last task on her bucket list, that meant keeping Lincoln Kolb in my sights.

And now, that's exactly where he is.

Not that I am going to act on it just yet, and not that Warchester is a bad school by any means. They have a decent photography major, and this semester there is even a visiting professor who worked for *National Geographic*. So I could kill two birds with one stone; focus on bettering my photography skills while also crossing off the biggest item on Catherine's list.

See, Catherine might have been my best friend, but it just so happens our houses stood next to each other, on the dividing lines of two towns. While I grew up in Little Port, Catherine lived in Winona Falls. Meaning we went to different schools, even if our bond was unbreakable.

Which meant we went to different high schools, and I wasn't present when Lincoln Kolb dumped her in front of the entire seventh-period lunch crowd a week after she told him she'd been diagnosed with cancer again. The fucker. I could literally go over there and wring his neck just thinking about it.

The anger in my bones over Catherine's death, over how unfair it is, still rages like a forest fire with no chance of being extinguished. And when I think about the guy who wronged her so horribly, who embarrassed her while her body began to fail on itself ... I understand now how people commit murder.

That's why I knew I had to come to Warchester. It sounded villainous, my plan, but it's not unlike anything Lincoln Kolb and all the other fuckboys out there like him have attempted. Manipulate the opposite sex into falling for them, falling into their bed, and then completely shatter their world when you admit that they were nothing but a hole and a good time.

Except I had to take this one step further. Catherine was half-blind for the guy, which means I have to make him fall in love with me. I have just enough piss and vinegar flowing through my veins to make it happen. There just needs to be a clear-cut plan, and then it should all fall into place.

Lincoln and his cronies are walking my way, making a beeline for the group of giggling freshman about to take their cover-ups off for all to see.

"Ladies, interested in a party tomorrow night?" The brawny, olive-skinned guy flanking Lincoln's right side says.

Lincoln's eyes are so wolfish as he approaches, I half expect him to start humping one of these willing participants right in front of the entire quad.

"Of course!" they all singsong in unison.

I have to try my best to swallow the snort. At least I can roll my eyes behind my sunglasses.

But talk of a party, now that has me interested. Scooting a little farther over on the bench, I listen in.

"It's at the football house over on Hudson, tomorrow night. Five dollars at the door for the keg, but mention my name, Lincoln Kolb, and I'll see what I can do for you."

God, he's so cocky. It's freaking irritating the way his voice, smooth like the first cup of morning coffee, slides down my spine. It's deep and just a little bristled, and clearly, I'm not the only one affected.

"Well, we'll just have to see what we can do for you." A brunette in a cherry red bikini leers at him.

Jesus Christ.

"What's your favorite drink?" The other guy walking with them, another football bro, can't tear his eyes away from the girl in the white two piece's ass.

I mean, it's pretty hard for everyone's eyes not to direct there, it's a piece of dental floss thong that I wouldn't even dare wear on a nudist beach in the South of France.

"A buttery nipple," she deadpans, fluttering her eyelashes so many times it should knock an eyeball loose, and I almost have to applaud her.

That kind of sexual confidence in the middle of the afternoon with no drinks in one's system, that I know of, is bold. That level of obvious desperation is one I've heard about in college, but hadn't yet witnessed. This girl all but invited him to suck on her tits in the middle of the quad.

"Mine too. Or well, I prefer blow job shots most days. Or Jell-O shots, because I can work my fingers." He wiggles his digits in front of her face. And there you have it, folks.

If I didn't already think most men were perverts, and a lot of the chicks here wanted to land on their backs, I do now. I can't contain the snort that works its way through my throat and am not fast enough to swallow it.

The sound comes out, and I quickly redirect my sitting position, trying to look off in the other direction.

But then a shadow falls over me, and I know I've been busted.

"And what's your favorite drink?"

The timbre of his voice makes my teeth clank together, because goddamn it if I didn't just get a little wet.

Part of me keeps my vision directed down into the course catalog I have in my lap, pretending to not hear him.

"Let me guess. You're a white wine spritzer kind of girl." His tone is haughty and all-knowing, and I wish I could slam the thick spine of the book in my lap right into his crotch.

"Hm?" I ask, pretending to only just realize he's there, but not looking up.

From the corner of my eye, I see his foot tap once, then twice — an insecure tic. Pretty boy isn't used to being ignored.

"Your drink of choice? I'm asking because apparently buttery nipples and blow jobs don't seem to be your thing."

Neither of us miss the way he leaves the word shot off the end of both of those popular liquor drinks. And it should be illegal the way the word blow job sounds coming out of his mouth.

"Jim, Jack, or Johnny." I sneer up at him, too annoyed to care that he baited me.

And it's true. Growing up in a North Carolina town that was nearly on the cusp of being rural, my father taught me that you don't drink unless it's a strong whiskey. "It'll put hair on your chest," he always said, and I would cringe. Later on, after Catherine died and he snuck a fifth of Jack into my room, I understood why that was a good thing.

My hair and most of my face are shaded by the large sunhat I wore out here, along with the sunglasses obstructing his view of my face. I'm thankful I decided for an incognito look, not only because it makes me more mysterious, but because it gives me ample time to inspect the god-like specimen in front of me.

Lincoln Kolb ... shit, it should be a sin to look like this guy. You know when you read about guys in books or watch movies and they claim tall, dark and handsome? This guy exceeds all of those wimps by a hundred miles. His body is a mass of lean muscle, broad shoulders, tapered waist. His body is both the kind of pickup truck you want to get on your back in, and the sleek sports car that turns you on to the point of climbing over the gearshift.

He has thick chocolate-colored hair that usually falls past his shoulders; today it's up in a man bun. It shouldn't be attractive, but goddamn him, it's making my mouth water. Lincoln's face is all defined jaw and chiseled cheekbones, with one boyish dimple just barely there on the right cheek. Those lips are things women inject themselves with fillers to get, and then there is the ultimate panty slayer.

His eyes. One blue. One green. They're so brilliant and *interesting* that it's impossible not to get lost in them. And it's not even fair that they're rimmed with such thick, almost-black lashes, they put my own to shame.

I guess it doesn't suck that the guy I'm going to seduce and suck the life out of, like I'm a black widow spider, is fucking gorgeous. At the end of the day, good sex is a bonus and there is no way Lincoln Kolb could be bad. It would be such a damn shame.

I see him trying to check me out, to see what's going on under the hat, glasses, and loose sundress I'm sporting. I know my body is a good, no, great. I've always been pretty confident, and decent genes plus a love to lose myself in a run have served me well. I don't miss the way Lincoln's eyes blaze a trail up my bare legs.

"Well, Jimmy, maybe I'll see you at my party tomorrow night."

I guess I have a party to go to. Unfortunately for Lincoln Kolb, he has no idea the door he just openly invited me to walk through.

B y the time I make it back to my dorm room, my roommate has arrived.

I know this because as I stand outside my door, about to swipe my ID card to unlock the electronic lock, I can hear the bump of the bass from a Rick Ross song pounding through the metal. It's not my favorite type of music, but even I have to admit it has a certain swag that I can't help nodding my head to.

When I finally take a breath, knowing I'm going to encounter the human I'll be sharing space with for the next nine months, I open the door and walk in.

A very slim, taller than average girl with a waterfall of silky straight candy pink hair is standing on top of her designated bed, hanging a poster of Jimi Hendrix on the wall. Compared to my striped gray comforter and black-and-white photo print I took of the Venice Beach boardwalk when I visited California, her side of the room is bursting with color. A comforter that matches her hair, topped with lime green pillows. She's replaced her desk chair with one of those clear plastic chairs that looks like it's floating on air. There is a mass of photos of what must be her friends and family plastered to the wall above her desk, and another five classic album posters join Jimi Hendrix next to her bed.

"Hey," I throw out, hoping my voice carries over the Bose speaker vibrating on her desk.

She whips around, and I'm struck by the teal blue nose ring and gorgeous, cat-like features.

"Oh, hi! I didn't hear you come in. Shit, sorry if this is too loud!" She scrambles down and somehow makes it look graceful.

My roommate looks like Misty Copeland, beautifully long limbs and soft, darkened skin. Her finger slams down on the volume button on her speaker as she smiles at me sheepishly.

"No worries at all, it's a good song." I nod, trying to sound cool.

In all honesty, I just want this to be easy. Going in, I knew I probably wouldn't find my next Catherine. Shit, just thinking the thought feels like a slap across my own face. The sting of losing her, of disrespecting her memory or replacing her ... I hate it. But I do need this to work. I need my roommate to be relaxed and not get in my way on the quest to ruining Lincoln Kolb's life. And not having to tiptoe around a person I'm living with would be a nice bonus.

"Sweet. I'm Rhiannon." She sticks out a hand, and I notice her nails are the exact same shade as her nose ring.

For someone who appreciates color ratios and odd pairings, I would love to take a photo series on my new roommate. Not many people could pull off these color combos so boldly, and with such grace, but Rhiannon does.

I shake her extended fingers. "Henley. I hope it's okay I took that side of the room."

She shrugs. "Totally cool, I'm really not picky. Except about my music. Do you like rap? Because if not, we're going to have a problem."

Part of me can't help but laugh at the way she states her preference as if it's a fact everyone should live by. I think I'm going to like this girl.

"I like it, although I'll tell you now I'm not super educated on it. I'm more of an easy listening slash pop girl myself, but I can hang." God, I sound like a seventy-year-old grandmother who doesn't know how to use Spotify.

Rhiannon nods, assessing me. "We can work with that. By the end of this school year, you'll have at least four Tupac songs memorized."

"Goody." I half laugh, half roll my eyes.

Our cinderblock dorm room looks like a picture in opposites. Rhiannon is a pastel and neon cloud of color, where my side is pretty stark of any personal touches and done in swatches of gray and white. Somehow, it kind of works. We're in one of the nicer dorms on campus, and thank goodness this floor isn't co-ed because there is something disgusting about sharing a public bathroom with boys.

"So, what's your story, Henley? Do you despise color or something?" She's surprisingly upfront, and it catches me off guard.

I haven't encountered many girls like myself over the years. I'm no-nonsense, bullshit-proof, and rarely take a liking to someone at first impression. I'm not sure why, I had a good childhood and plenty of positive reinforcement. Maybe it's just how I'm programmed. Aside from Catherine, I only had surface friends back in my hometown.

Which makes part of this whole scheming to break Lincoln Kolb's heart thing sit uneasy in my stomach. I'm not a liar. Hell, I can barely let a white lie slip when someone asks if something looks good on them and I know it doesn't. Or when my mom asks if dinner is good, I have to bite my tongue and plant a super fake smile on my face … lord, the woman is an angel in many areas but food is not one of them.

But the final task on Catherine's bucket list requires almost undercover-level disguise; I'm not this person, I don't con other people from the truth ever. Yet this asks for so much deceit.

"I'm a photography major, and I love black-and-white subjects. It's a weakness that unfortunately seeps into my closet and design choices." I shrug.

There, that wasn't a lie. At least with Rhiannon, I can attempt to be myself.

She nods. "I dig that. Honestly, it kind of suits you. So, photography major, that makes sense. How long did it take you to get here?"

"About an hour? I live in North Carolina, so pretty close by. How about you? And what're you studying?" I flop down on my bed as she walks to her clear desk chair, folding her long limbs into a yoga-like pose.

"I'm from Florida. Took me a plane to get here. But this was the best recording industry program on the East Coast that I could get into, so here I am." Rhiannon starts flipping through vinyls she retrieves from a bag.

"So you want to go into music?" I assume.

She shakes her head. "Nope. I want to find musicians. The next Beyoncé. The next Bruno Mars. I have an ear for this thing. I know everyone trying to muscle their way into A & R says that same thing, but I swear it's like my sixth sense."

I've only known her for a few minutes, but I'm inclined to believe her. "That sounds like such a cool job."

"And a hard one. It'll take a lot of blood and sweat, and maybe a few blow jobs, to get where I want," she deadpans.

It takes a second for the slow smile to spread over her lips, and then we both crack up at her sardonic joke. Honestly, her climb into music manager stardom sounds a little like my mission to make this college's big man on campus fall in love with me.

"Anything else I should know? Jealous boyfriend from home who will be visiting? Do you smoke?" She eyes me, half-joking.

I hold my hands, as if I have nothing to hide. "No boyfriend, men are horrible beings. I don't smoke, unless you're into a weed brownie now and then. In that case, I'm down. I don't snore, or I haven't been told I do. I binge seasons of *Vampire Diaries* and *Parks & Rec*, although I've seen them all already. And I will always be in for a late-night taco order."

Rhiannon walks over to me, extending her hand for a high five. "My girl. Tacos are the thing that will bond us, of this I'm sure. As long as you like extra hot sauce on yours."

"Wouldn't have them any other way," I second.

Walking back to her side, she pulls a bottle from the depths of her suitcase. "So, when are we getting drunk?"

"I do have this party we could go to ..."

T he house feels like it's on fire.

An inferno licks up my back as I make my way through the mass of sweaty bodies, noise, and heat and confusion coming from every angle. It's the best kind of chaos, but fuck, didn't someone think to open a window or crank the air up?

"Linc, grab me a beer!" Derrick calls through the noise, a girl's ass pinned to his front.

I already have about three shots of bourbon in me, and I'm feeling loose, but in control. Technically, this isn't my house yet, and I don't want to make an ass out of myself in front of the upperclassmen. Especially since I'm the young guy coming in trying to be their driving force, their in-all-but-the-title captain. As a freshman, I won't get that title. But as their soon-to-be quarterback, I need their respect.

It doesn't mean I can't have a great time, though. The amount of hot girls here tonight, some that would literally drop to their knees to service one of the guys on the football team, is insane. I've never seen so many beautiful women in a room together. And aside from that, there is an epic game of beer pong

I'm about to start running on a table in the living room. My best friends are here, and I'm bonding with other guys on the team.

College is so fucking awesome.

Walking to the kitchen to grab Derrick and myself large cups of foamy beer, I can't help but drink in all the chicks barely covered in scraps of clothing. My dick tingles in anticipation; it's been a month and a half of long preseason hours and no hot sex. I feel like a goddamn celibate, and I know many of the guys on the team feel the same as well. It'll be a fuck fest in here tonight for sure, and I can say with one hundred percent certainty that I'm bringing one of these fine ladies back to my dorm room tonight.

When I finally make it to the keg, lots of suggestive glances following me, I pull two red cups from the stack and cut the line. No one protests, I'm already a known face and name here. I don't plan on abusing that privilege, but I'm next up on the beer pong table and I don't plan on missing that opportunity.

It's not until a swath of golden hair and the scent of spicy citrus catches me that I pause, looking over the girl next up in line.

"Want a beer, sweetheart?" I puff my chest out at the blonde waiting for the keg.

She slants me a look that says *Don't use a nickname on me, buddy*, and then her lips curl up in a sneer.

"I thought I told you I only drink the three strongest men in the bunch."

Fuck, her voice. Like smoky heat that licks right down to my balls. It's gravelly with a hint of sweet, just like the top-shelf whiskey she's mentioned. I want to drink from her lips, to hear that voice moan my name as I'm buried fully inside her.

And if just this girl's voice can have me sporting a semi despite the shots of bourbon I've already downed, then her face could make me come on sight. She's an absolute knockout. All tanned tight curves like one of those girls who's into hot yoga and working their ass on the stair stepper. She's average in height, which means I have to tip my chin a fair amount down to peer into her cleavage, but I've never cared about coming off as a leerer. They're great tits, full and perky, and she's showcased them in a tight white dress that leaves little to the imagination. I wish I could ask her to turn around, because her ass has to be equally as great.

She has these full, cherry-red lips that are almost too big for her face. Dick sucking lips, if I've ever seen them. Light brown eyes, the color of the sweetest kind of tea on a hot summer afternoon. A beauty mark just above her upper lip on the left side. And that hair. Fucking hell, that hair. Thick and falling in ropes of unruly blond curls down her back. Most of the girls in here have tamed their hairs with hours of those dildo looking tools they store in their bathroom, but you can tell this one kept it all natural. I want this mass of curls around my fist. I want it falling over my chest as she rides me.

Then it clicks.

"You're the girl from the quad. The one who snorts at buttery nipples."

This description makes her crack a smile. "I can't say it's the worst moniker ever, but it will be sure to turn some heads if I introduce myself like that in my classes."

Wit. I like wit. My dick stirs even more, because if this girl can actually hold her own against my ego, the sex might be that much more incredible.

"You could just tell me your name, Jimmy." I quirk an eyebrow, giving her my best cocky smile.

Her caramel eyes twinkle as we spar with words. "A lady never introduces herself first."

Someone behind her clears their throat, clearly anxious to make it to the keg, and I take the opportunity to touch her. With my hand on her back, I gently nudge us to the side. We stand in a mostly empty party of the kitchen, some of the noise filtered out by the ancient wood paneling on the walls.

The football house has seen better days, and someone could have said that same thing twenty years ago. In all honesty, the house is disgusting. It's a party shack filled with amenities to host better parties. A two-story beer bong that snakes through the front hallway from the balcony above. Giant speakers in the living room, connected to a DJ booth that stays up all hours of the day and days of the week. Mattresses in the basement for ... guests. I don't even want to know what's on those, but there are people desperate enough for a bone that will go down there and use them.

"That was bold." My new curly girl smirks.

"Huh?" I say, lost in her eyes and lips now that we're so close.

"Touching a girl without permission. In this day and age, I could probably have you tarred and feathered for that."

"Tarred and feathered." I can't help but let a laugh boom out of my throat. "Who even says that?"

She crosses her arms over her chest, which only serves to draw my attention to her chest more than it already was. "I do."

"I think I deserve to know the name of a girl who speaks like a nineteen hundreds southern belle." I wink, knowing that my charm is dialed all the way up.

Now she smirks, unable to contain her smile, although I can tell she doesn't want to let it slip. "And I didn't know hulking jocks even knew what southern belles spoke like in the nineteen hundreds. I'm a woman by the way, and my name is Henley."

Ah, I got her. Determined now, from her answer, I push forward. "So, you know I'm a jock?"

"We're at a football party, and you cut the line for the keg. Either you have a death wish, or you're one of the chosen ones here." Henley scowls, and I think idly that her name is far too pretty for a girl with such a saucy mouth.

Henley sounds like the name of a woodland fairy, or a princess in one of those paranormal movies. This blond bomb-shell looks like she could fight an entire kingdom of douchy jocks, and it makes her that much more tempting.

"Lincoln Kolb, quarterback." I extend a hand with a shit-eating grin on my face.

Henley eyes it as if I might have had that hand up another girl's skirt tonight, but then finally shakes it. The moment our palms touch, a sizzle runs from my fingers up my arm and vibrates out to my entire body.

"Henley Rowan, hater of buttery nipples." Her gorgeous round eyes crinkle with sarcastic laughter.

"Play pong with me," I offer, not letting her hand go but mentally kicking myself.

I promised Janssen we'd run the table, and it's always a bad move to try to seduce the chick you're trying to bang by offering up a pity game of beer pong. Chicks were never as good as me, *especially* me, and we'd most certainly lose.

But I know that if I walk away from Henley right now, I won't find her again.

"Can't. I'm here with my roommate." She shrugs as if she has no problem saying no to me.

That doesn't happen often. "Tell her to join us."

The innuendo isn't lost on Henley, and she narrows her eyes. "I'm not sure where ..."

She trails off and swings her gaze in the direction of the DJ booth as the song changes. A slamming rap beat powers through my chest, and when I follow her line of sight, I see a sexy as fuck pink-haired girl all but pushing Kenny, our desig-nated beat master, out of the booth.

"That your roommate? Looks occupied to me," I whisper smugly in her ear.

I don't miss the shiver that moves down her back at my proximity.

Swatting me like an annoying fly, she capitulates. "Fine. But no one is taking any clothes off. It's not that kind of game. And try to keep up. I don't want to make the new quarterback look like his arm is weak as shit."

I lag behind her for a second, a laugh caught in my throat, as I watch what just might be the feistiest creature on two long tan legs stalk toward the pong table.

Oh, *hell* yes. This night just started getting good.

* * *

Two hours later, after we've dominated five games of beer pong, danced until my cock couldn't take the friction any longer, and downed a secret bottle of Johnny Walker I'd stashed in the fridge, I finally convince Henley to leave the party with me.

I'm halfway to desperate that I consider bringing her to the basement, but this is the kind of girl that, once I get her naked, I plan to have my way with a number of times. I want her in my bed; I want privacy and space to taste every inch of her, multiple times.

That's what I feel like doing with this mystery of a woman who beat every opponent in pong and scored more shots per game than even I did. She wasn't lying when she said I should keep up. I'm almost contemplating whether she shouldn't be playing for our university team.

Henley is magnetic, with her flirty eye contact, slim curves, cool-girl persona and overall badassness. I couldn't have picked a better chick to end my celibate streak with.

She lets me grasp her waist as we walk, the drinks in us making us sway and giggle. Her skin smells like freshly squeezed oranges, maybe the blood red kind because Henley has this sort of spice or zest about her. I can't get close enough to her, yet she's an enigma. Either shrugging me off or coming so close that her lips all but brush my jaw.

I can tell she's baiting me, but I don't fucking care. I could have taken any girl at that party home, but this is the one I know will be ... well, fucking orgasmic. Since she told me off at the keg, even in the quad yesterday, I could tell there was a chemistry that would make sex between us one of the funnest things I've done in a while. Getting off is great, but having a rowdy, sweaty time while doing it makes it all that much more satisfying.

The two towers that flank either side of the quad we cross into stand like gleaming beams in the night. They're made up of twelve floors each, filled with horny and drunk students at this hour. Certain rooms are lit up as we stare into the night, others are dark. Whether that's due to hooking up going on inside, or the roomies still being at various parties throughout town, your guess has a fifty-fifty chance of being correct.

"I'm in East tower," she says, her unruly curls flashing in the glints of moonlight.

"I'm in West. I think you should come to West tonight." Wrapping my arms around her waist, I finally pin her into place.

My tongue darts out, licking my own lips, as I gaze at hers. Shit, I'm really into this. I want to know what she tastes like.

"And yet, I think I should go into East. Alone. Seeing as how I just met you. I don't even know your middle name." Henley gives me a sardonic grin and wiggles out of my embrace.

My hand trails down her arm, lacing my fingers through hers when it reaches them as I refuse to let her go easily. "It's Stallion," I joke. "Come to East tower and I'll show you why."

Henley cringes as she laughs. "God, that was cheesy. Does that usually work for you?"

I shrug. "Usually, I don't have to work at all."

She's silent for a moment, our eyes locking in a battle of wills and something ... bigger.

"Good night, *Stallion*." Breaking our interlaced hands, she brushes her nail over my bicep, and the sensation causes all the hairs on my neck to stand up.

As she struts away, a slow, swaggering thrust of her hips to each side, I can't help but thrust a fist in my mouth. Fuck, that ass beneath me would have been the best kind of reward tonight. She thinks she won this round, and maybe she did. Henley has the upper hand, but I don't admit defeat for very long. If ever.

"See you soon, Jimmy," I call after her.

The nickname causes her to stutter, and it's such a small movement that she thinks I don't notice. I do.

As I walk away, backward so I can make sure she gets inside —and also watch her ass shimmy—I like to think that she's wearing a goofy grin because of me.

5

HENLEY

T he bright openness of Warchester's communications building mesmerizes me as I push through the doors.

Even though it isn't my top choice, I have to admit, the draw of the communications school is a strong one. Warchester's Parc School of Communications is top rated in the state, not to mention the country. It has a ton of grants for student projects, a TV/radio program that feeds directly into two of the highest rated cable stations in the world, and a photography studio that I could live in if it wasn't frowned upon.

My schedule is chock-full of photography classes, both theory and mechanics as well as live subject courses. And for the first time in the last few months, I can immerse myself in my favorite thing on earth. When I'm behind the lens of a camera, the rest of the world falls away. Whether I'm capturing human subjects, landscapes, or just wandering while capturing life in motion, it all lights my soul on fire. I get to take a snapshot in time, give life to a moment or a feeling that could impact those that view it for decades to come.

I know a lot of students avoid the eight a.m. courses, but I'm a morning person. And being in this building during a slow time of day is pretty darn peaceful. Sunlight spills through the wall of windows that makes up the front of the communications school, while art deco chairs are grouped into clusters around solid wood coffee tables. Classroom doors flank the hallways farther in, and flat-screens hang on every wall, displaying student video, journalism, or photography work.

Checking the schedule written in my planner, I locate room 423 and enter. I'm one of the first students to arrive in Photography Through the Ages, so I pull out my phone to check my messages. I threw it in the front pocket of my cognac leather backpack this morning, along with the bucket list Catherine wrote. It might sound dumb, me carrying it around, but I wanted to have a piece of her with me on my first day of college classes. After all, this would have been the place she attended college.

Typing in my passcode, my cell comes to life, the photo of the white deer I took in my parent's backyard the background on my phone. I have no messages, no missed calls, and one notification on Facebook. Opening the app, I see that Rhiannon has tagged me in yet another photo she's posted to social media. My roommate has a curated feed, along with her flawless Instagram, and she makes me look good in even the earliest of morning selfies. This morning, she insisted we snap a pic together before heading off to our first classes at Warchester. Her bubble gum locks are smooshed up against my unruly curls, and I look happy but plain next to her.

Other than that, I don't have any new activity on my feed. I half expected Lincoln Kolb to stalk me, friend request me, or get my number from someone who does those kinds of things for the jocks on this campus.

I have him right where I want him. Well, not entirely, but it was a damn good start. I had him eating out of the palm of my hand, there is no doubt that when I agreed to leave the party with him, he thought I'd be on my back, in his bed, underneath him. God, part of me had wanted to do it. To catch him hook, line, and sinker, because I'm great in bed. Sure, I've only had two partners, but I enjoyed myself, tried some sexy things and only had shouts of satisfaction at the end.

Another part of me wanted to know what it would be like, sex with Lincoln. I know what I'm on this mission for, but having sex with one of the most gorgeous male specimens I've ever encountered isn't a terrible side perk. He's got to be fantastic, I can tell by the shit-eating, cocky grin he had on his face most of the night.

But it's too soon. Give the milk away for free, without strings attached, and he'll never buy the cow. And by the time I'm done with him, Lincoln will be paying for this woman like I'm Kobe beef.

"This seat taken?" someone asks, and I pull my bag off the table space in front of the empty chair.

"Nope," I say hastily, scooting to let them into the seat.

The room is not unlike any of my high school classrooms, save for the smart board and the community table. It's shaped like a half-moon, with about twenty chairs pushed in around it. Aside from me and my new neighbor, there has to be maybe a dozen other students who've filed in.

"I'm Jamie." The girl who sits down next to me smiles.

She's got this gorgeous auburn bob and sparkling green eyes. Part of me wants to get her in the sunlight and photograph the glint on her irises. That's how my brain works, which I guess is kind of weird. Jamie has freckles across her cheeks and nose, and she's pulling a leather-bound notebook from her black satchel.

"Henley." I nod. "You're a photography major?"

I can't assume everyone in here is, because this is just an

intro class and I'm sure people think it will be easy when they see it in the course catalog.

She shakes her head. "No, I'm undecided. But I've always liked the idea of photography, and so I thought I'd give this class a shot. How about you?"

Part of me bristles. It sours my mood to hear that people just want to *give photography a shot* when it's the thing I've strived to do since my parents bought me my first DSLR. But I guess I can't fault her, and I actively choose to shoo the thought from my brain. Catherine always did say I was too negative.

"Sounds like a good plan. I'm a photographer, through and through. If my parents didn't insist on me earning a college degree, I would have just started my own business and begun shooting weddings or something."

Jamie smiles. "Well, then we'll have to partner up when we study. That or I'll just copy off your test. But I make a mean cookie, so you may want to consider the teammate offer."

I'm usually a lone wolf, hence why photography is my chosen passion. I operate in a solitary manner, not answering to anyone or having to go by another's schedule. But something in me, or maybe because Catherine's list is in my bag, makes me bend.

"Cookies are a form of payment in my book. You've got a deal."

Just then, the room goes from a dull roar of conversation to almost silent, and the professor walks to the front of the room.

"Please, don't stop on my account. Seriously, guys, this is college. Not high school. I'm not your overlord, and I don't care what you call me as long as it isn't Professor or Mr. Mullins. Kyle, please. So I guess, just call me Kyle."

Kyle, as I shall now refer to him, looks like he was plucked out of a Brooklyn coffee shop. He's probably in his mid-thirties, with tight black skinny jeans, a white T-shirt that probably cost a hundred dollars, and a ratty beanie cap even though it's almost ninety degrees outside. He's trying to give off this relaxed, easy guy vibe and I hope to God that it's actually real. And that he actually knows his shit when it comes to photography.

"I know we have some specified photography majors in this class, and some who are considering declaring. This course is going to be a comprehensive lesson in this mode of art through the ages. Just so we all get to know each other, and you assume I know what I'm doing, I was a travel photographer for over a decade before going into teaching. I was the resident photographer at an elephant sanctuary in Thailand, traveled the Alps over a six-month period for a BBC project, and visited Barbados during Carnival to do a piece for *Travel & Leisure*."

Well, shit, this guy just proved that he knows his stuff in about twelve seconds flat. And with the publications he's tied to, he probably has some great internship connections.

The Warchester photography program just got a whole lot more intriguing.

6

LINCOLN

"Second team, you're up!"

Coach Daniels's voice booms across the practice field and I jog hastily out, head angled down as if I'm about to fully charge an impending army.

I may be second team today, but with the aggression and determination in my muscles and bones, that won't last for long. We've been out here for almost two hours already, watching the first team run through drills. It's true what they say, that everything gets bigger as you move up. The playbooks are thicker; the linemen are scarier, the wide receivers seem to jump all the way to the moon.

Good thing football is my lifeblood. It's the thing I care most about in this world. Since the second I picked up the oblong, brown leather ball with its white stitches when I was five years old, this has been it for me. The smell of the turf sprinkled with morning dew. The way it burns off in the heat so that the wavy lines look like a mirage in the desert when you look across it. Each thud of a practice pad, or clink of a helmet as the strap is popped in. The intricate, almost dance-like routine of each play, of each option to that play.

"Kolb, I want to see that arm. Let's run some different routes, and lob 'em out there," Coach says.

I've envisioned playing for Coach Walter Daniels since I was a boy. He's the most winningest coach in all of North Carolina and has been for the last decade. In terms of college football, he's brought six national championship trophies back to Warchester, and has produced countless big league players in his almost fifteen years of coaching this team. The man demands excellence, but I've heard he isn't unreasonable and harsh like some other coaches are rumored to be when you get to this level.

"Yes, sir." I nod my head, ready to show them all what I can do.

My confidence in my abilities is unwavering. Not only do I know I'm the best, but I put the practice where my mouth is. I'm the first one in, last one out. I carry equipment the same as everyone else, do extra reps in the weight room, and memorize the playbook until I can write each one out without my notes. In order to be the best, you have to be the best at everything in this sport. So, I am. And yes, I have an ego. But it only serves to make me better. If you don't think you're the best, why the hell would other people think that?

"Matthews, down the field." Coach points his finger all the way to the end zone of the practice field.

Archie Matthews, a junior and arguably the best wide receiver in the college ranks currently, takes off in a sprint down the field. I get in position, eyeing him and the center about to spike the ball to me. Being a quarterback is all about multi-tasking, remembering your plays, reading the field, watching the defense, and throwing the ball where it's supposed to be before your teammate even gets there.

And by the time the ball is in my hands, my fingers flexing

like they've done thousands of times over the stitches, I know right where Archie will be when he needs to turn over his back shoulder and catch the ball. My sixth sense tingles and I launch my left arm back, all the tendons and muscles trained on exactly how to launch the perfect spiral. Without another thought, I let it go, a smug grin coming over my lips as it sails through the air.

At the moment I predicted he would, Archie turns, his foot crossing the line into the end zone, and the football lands perfectly in his hands. He secures it, burns off the sprint, and then jumps up.

"Woo, that boy has an arm!" Archie, who is about a head taller than my six-two frame, claps his massive hands around the ball.

I give him a nod like I know that I do, and I can feel the eyes on me. I've got their attention now.

After throwing at least two dozen more routes with different spins, options, and fakes, I miss all but two. It helps that these are some of the best receivers and tight ends in the country; Warchester only recruits the best.

Practice is called a little after that, and we're all dripping sweat. It's one of the last afternoons in a North Carolina August, and damn does it feel like the pits of hell.

"I have so much jock itch, my balls need an ice bath." Archie walks funny as he falls in line with Derrick and me.

"Dude, tell me about it. Not to mention, my cup is two sizes too small. Gotta ask them about getting me a magnum cup." Janssen smirks as he walks backward in front of us to face our trio.

Derrick throws a towel at his face. "Shut the fuck up. We all know you're sporting a roll of pennies in there. Remember that brunette he got with?"

"The townie?" I snicker, because Janssen had been so fucked

up he didn't realize he was trying to bang a cougar maybe fifteen years older than us.

"Yep." Derrick nods. "He could barely get it up."

Janssen scowls. "I had five shots of whiskey, no shit I couldn't get hard."

"It happens to the best of us, my friend." Archie claps him on the shoulder. "Just not me. Or any red-blooded male I know."

We all crack up at my best friend's expense, until Coach Daniels interrupts us. From across the field, he calls my name and waves a hand, ushering me over.

"Catch you guys later," I say to the group, then jog to where Coach stands.

"Good work out there today, Kolb. You've got a good arm, but we can improve your footwork. I'd like to start working you in with some of the first team guys, so tell Phil tomorrow that you'll be shadowing them."

Phil is the team's offensive coordinator, and rumor was he was getting called up to the big leagues next year.

"Thank you, Coach. I look forward to learning and getting more starts." I don't leave that part out, because we both know I'm gunning for the job.

"Being a great football player doesn't mean anything if you don't act like a leader. I'm not saying you've shown me otherwise, but I expect my players to be both good athletes and great men alike. Nice work today; hit the showers."

He dismisses me and I'm smart enough not to say more.

I'm behind the team, so by the time I take my shower and throw on clothes to head to class, I'm the last one out. It's nice to have the quiet, to not have to shoot the shit or pretend to be macho for a minute. I thrive in groups, but sometimes being alone is what I need.

I'm headed to my play and leisure course, which sounds like a lot of bullshit, but is required for my physical education teaching major. That's right. My fallback is becoming a gym teacher. Which, let's face it, is never going to happen. I can't think it actually will. I'm going to be playing football until my body gives out on me, which is hopefully twenty years from now. Any other outcome is not acceptable.

Across the quad, I spot a familiar figure. Crouched down low, with an old-school camera pressed against her face, is Henley. Her curls are piled in a mass on her head, secured by two pencils, and fuck, if that isn't the sexiest thing I've ever seen. Just pulling one out like a Jenga piece would make the whole thing unravel, and wouldn't that be a sight to see?

She's snapping away, of what I'm guessing are shots of the quad. What does she see? And why does she have to have that sexy pout, like she's chewing on her tongue, while she does it? I suddenly have the urge to chew on that tongue.

"Henley Rowan." I whistle in a low, appreciative tone as I walk to her.

Her head snaps up from her camera screen, and I see it in her eyes, that split second of panic. She's contemplating making a run for it. And then, in the next breath, she's cooling her features. More than likely, she thinks I didn't see that. This is a girl not used to being caught off guard, and I like that I rattle her.

Those full cherry lips slide into a smirk. "Lincoln Kolb, what a surprise. I thought they keep you in the locker room and only take you out for games. Wasn't aware you actually knew how to get to academic buildings."

"Oh no, they let us out to eat and fornicate, too." I wink.

Her eyes flash with amusement. "Good to know. Go on, fornicate. I'm busy with something."

The nails on her hands are polished a dark purple gray, and they twist different buttons and circles on her camera.

"You like photography?" I venture a guess.

Not sure why I'm asking. Maybe it's another way to get her to come up to my dorm room. Because damn, with a mouth that can verbally spar that well, I need to know what it can really do in the bedroom.

Her whiskey-colored eyes roll so hard, I'm afraid they might fall out of her head. "I don't *like* photography. It's my career. My passion. The thing I want to do with my life."

That honest answer hits me like a punch to the gut. Since I've known this girl, she's done nothing but flirt with, chastise, and taunt me. Hearing the thing that she loves most ... well, it's like football for me. I get it; I get that soul deep need to do it.

"What were you taking photos of? What out here is interesting?" Suddenly, I'm invading her space, sitting on the bench she and her equipment are occupying.

Henley grabs at her lenses and the bag they go in, acting like my grubby paws might break one. "You wouldn't get it."

And just like that, I'm shut out. But I don't go down that easily. No, something about this girl has wedged itself under my skin. And whether she be a splinter or the warm fuzzies, I want to know why.

"Well, you can't sit out here and play paparazzi forever. Why don't you—"

Just as I'm about to swoop in for the kill, convincing her to have lunch in the dining hall with me, my phone vibrates at my thigh.

Shit. Nine times out of ten, if I'm in a situation where my penis will be rewarded, I'd ignore it. But as I glance at the screen and it reads Dad, I know I can't just send it to voice mail. There was a hearing today, and I want to know what the outcome of it was.

"You know what? I have to run. Maybe I'll see you around, Jimmy." I use the nickname I gave her back on the first day we met.

Henley looks a little shocked before I turn on my heel and walk off, and maybe it's a good thing I had a call come in.

Because I think I just took that upper hand back.

7

HENLEY

S taring at the box of hair dye in my hands, my mind starts to go into panic mode.

"I really don't want to do this," I tell Rhiannon as she snaps a rubber glove on her hand.

My roommate looks like she's about to give me a rectal exam, or maybe I just feel like that. I hate that Catherine had this on her bucket list, that I have to paint my virgin locks a different color.

But I made a commitment, and college rebellion and all that. Catherine would be proud of me; she could barely get me to put my curls through a straightener. Unlike ninety-nine percent of teenage and twenty-something girls, I have always loved my natural hair. The color, the thick, ropy curls, the way it seems to take on its own presence in humidity. I love my hair, and the fact that I'm about to dye it scarlet fever red, as the box says, really freaks me out.

"Oh, stop it. The dye will wash out in the shower tomorrow morning. You wouldn't even let me get the good stuff, so quit being such a chicken bitch." Rhiannon rolls her eyes.

In the week since classes have started, we've eaten almost all of our meals together, joined the *Habitat for Humanity* club on campus, and she's begun schooling me on all things hip-hop and R&B. I've really grown to like her; she both makes me laugh and doesn't put up with shit. We're very similar in our blunt approach, which normally doesn't work in a friendship, but for us, it does.

And forming a bond with Rhiannon only makes me miss Catherine more. What would our college years have been like? Visiting each other's schools, possibly studying abroad together, talking on FaceTime about our new crushes or how drunk we got last night. She knew me inside and out, and now that she's gone, it feels like an expanse has opened up in my chest. I'm not sure anyone or anything will ever be able to fill it.

"Okay, let's just do this before I change my mind." I blow out a long breath.

"Plus, think how amazing you'll look at the CEOs and hoes party. You'll be like that sexy secretary on *Mad Men*, with her silky red hair and huge tits." Rhiannon points a gloved finger at my chest.

"I don't have huge tits." I cross my arms over my chest, and it serves to highlight her point.

She raises one eyebrow as she shakes the dye bottle and squirts the first batch onto my scalp. It's cold on my skin, and I'm not sitting in front of the grungy mirror of our dorm room because I didn't want to watch this in real time.

"Um, honey, you have like Emily Ratajkowski tits. Perky, huge, stick out in that supermodel way from your chest kind of tits. It's no wonder football guy was trying to get into your bra at that last party."

"Who Lincoln?" I ask, trying to sound nonchalant.

"Um, yeah, *Lincoln*. I don't even like jocks, and I could drool over that. He's too much of a hunk, too meaty, for me, but damn, if he offered I'd probably take the ride for one go round. Why didn't you jump on that? You know I would be cool with a scrunchie on the door."

I feel it as Rhiannon slathers another goopy hand on my head. She works the dye into my roots, down my long, long locks, and I can feel this side of me come out. When I wash this out, when I let her style my hair, I'll look like a completely different person. Along with the high-waisted black lace underwear, no bra, and oversized suit jacket I'll be wearing with black pumps tonight; Lincoln Kolb won't know what hit him.

Theme parties have never been my thing, but tonight, a racy thrill runs up my spine. It feels naughty to be so bad, so secretive and deceptive. That sounds terrible, but a dark part of me is really enjoying this.

He tripped me up, and he knows it. I was too busy and hyped up about my first photography assignment for Kyle's class, that I didn't notice him. I didn't have my game face on. And for that, I'm pissed at myself. Yes, photography is what I want to do with my life, but I need to finish Catherine's list on my way there. This is the top priority right now, and the fact that he just got under my skin really frustrates me.

But tonight, I'm going to change all that. I have to bring in the big guns, and a themed party with lots of alcohol is just the way to do that.

"Oh, would you? Does that mean I can expect a scrunchie on the door?" I look back, raising an eyebrow at her.

She smirks. "Maybe. I have this guy back home though ... it's kind of on and kind of off. He may come visit, but we haven't ironed out the details. So, no, I guess no random scrunchies, but I'll tell you if there is a scheduled scrunchie."

"Oh, I want to see a picture of this on-and-off boy. But to answer, maybe. Maybe I'll put a scrunchie on the door. Though, I don't like to shit where I sleep."

This makes Rhiannon laugh so hard, she snorts. "Girl, I knew I liked you."

I nod. "It's easier to do my business, get my orgasm, and be on my way. If the guy is clingy, or worse, *drunk*, then he stays the night in your bed. Those extra-long twins are small as it is, so *hell no* do I want a sweaty dude smelling of alcohol hogging my cover."

At this point, I almost have Rhiannon in tears. "Jesus, you're like one of those bugs who eats its young."

"Just honest." I shrug.

"All right, honesty queen. Time to rinse this out. And then, I'm going full curling wand on your ass."

Oh, goody. Can't wait to see how different I look. At least it'll take Lincoln by surprise and possibly give me the upper hand.

There are way too many dudes in pimp hats here. I'm not sure who thought a CEO wore a black top hat, but someone here clearly sent a memo and these frat bros and jocks took notice in full force. Shirtless guys in tux pants, girls in librarian skirts with bras and fake glasses—this surely is a theme party at its best.

And after slamming a tequila shot with Rhiannon immediately after walking through the doors of this random frat house off campus, I'm ready to find the target of my mission.

Lincoln stands along the wall, talking to a group mixed with both guys and girls. He's edible in black fitted suit pants and a white button-down that has two too many buttons open. An untied tie hangs from the collar, and he looks like his secretary just fucked him on top of his desk.

The thought has me squeezing my thighs together, and the

friction is so delicious. It's been since before Catherine's funeral that I hooked up with anyone, and my horny meter is at its peak.

Sauntering over, I can feel the eyes on my tits. They're bouncing free, everything above my navel visible in this oversized suit jacket. Thank God for double-sided tape.

I wiggle into the group until I'm pressed against the wall next to him. Either he didn't notice my arrival or he's already too drunk to care, but Lincoln doesn't even look my way.

"Hey, Stallion," I say, only for him to hear.

His head turns, taking me in. Those eyes, one blue and one green, have no hint of familiarity there. He drinks in my face, my hair, my cleavage, and down to the six-inch heels Rhiannon convinced me were a good idea.

"Holy shit ... Henley?" His face lowers closer to mine, his lips just inches from my mouth.

I nod, a smug smile gracing my lips. "Did I catch you off guard?"

This was my plan. Throw him for a loop, make everything about me unpredictable. Because if there is one thing guys like Lincoln love, it's an unpredictable girl. They love the chase, the adventure, the insanity. How fun is it to be with a girl you're not sure will remain the same in the next second?

"Your hair. It's ... different." He eyes me skeptically, and suddenly, we're not standing in the group anymore.

I'm not sure when he gently pushed me farther down the wall, so we could be in our own little bubble. But when I glance up, his elbow is propped against the wall, shutting the rest of the party out.

I nod, because boys are morons when it comes to noticing beauty trends. "It is."

"I don't like it," Lincoln states matter-of-factly.

My jaw drops a little with shock and at his rude bluntness.

"And that's supposed to matter? Last time I checked, you have no say over what I do. With my body or otherwise."

I feel my blood pulse with rage. How dare this scum of a human, who dumped my best friend over cancer, make comments about my appearance?

Lincoln reaches out, his large hand catching my elbow. The touch sends lust plummeting low in my belly, and I hate both of us for it.

"Henley, that's not what I meant. It looks great, anything would look great on you. I just ... I love your hair. All of those blond curls. I'll miss them."

And there, in the middle of a noisy, rambunctious college party, Lincoln Kolb melts a piece of my frigid heart. He used my name; he complimented me on something I love about myself. And even though he's only met me a handful of times, he's claiming he'll miss them, which implies he's going to see me again.

I get it now, why he's so dangerous. This charm, whether it's an act or the real thing, he's got it down to a science. The way he makes eye contact with one blue, one green, hypnotizing you into believing him. The small gentle touch, the whisper of his husky voice ...

He's a dangerous man, and I need to keep my head clear and my focus sharp.

I shake him off, the contact of his hand to my arm breaking. "It's temporary, should wash out in the shower. But, I think it's sexy. I'm thinking about keeping it."

"Everything you do is sexy. You don't have to worry about that." His eyes dilate, and I don't miss the way his tongue darts out to wet his lips.

The heat of his gaze is like a branding iron moving down the center of my chest, and when he leans over on his tiptoes, I swear I feel the shadow of his fingers skimming my most private parts.

"Well, I enjoy being someone different, even if it's just for the night. How about I show you who I am?"

My intention coming into this party was to get physical with Lincoln. It was time. If I held out for too long, some other girl would come along and suck his dick. Boys like this are easily distracted. But if I gave in too soon, agreeing to make on base, any base, the first time we met well, my plan would have been over before it even started.

Without letting Lincoln get another word in, I grab his hand, our fingers lacing. Anticipation flutters in my stomach as I locate the stairs in search of, at least, an unoccupied bathroom.

If one of the bedrooms is unlocked, that'll be even better.

As soon as we make it to the top of the stairs, Lincoln is all over me.

From behind, his big hands wrap around my waist, kneading at the suit jacket covering my skin. I melt into him, wanting nothing more than to grind against the erection I feel so rigid at my back. If I don't find us a private space in the next three seconds, we'll be giving whoever floats up here from the party below a show.

Giggling and moaning as Lincoln affixes his mouth to my neck, nibbling the skin there, I move awkwardly with him at my back. Jiggling each door handle as we move farther down the hall, each one not budging an inch. About three doors from the end of the hallway, one finally gives way, and we stumble into a small full bathroom.

The sink and toilet are practically on top of each other, and I don't even want to open the shower curtain to reveal the disgusting boy filth inside. But at this point, I couldn't care less. My heart is pumping an overload of lust into my veins, and that thing that Lincoln is doing to my ear has white spots popping at the edges of my vision.

Turning at the same time he pulls me flush up against him, I'm ready to explore all the dangerous that is Lincoln Kolb. The bastard is grinning right before his lips descend on mine, and in the split second before he kisses me, I put my brain in check.

This is for Catherine. I will not develop feelings for this man. Sex and connection are separate entities, and Lincoln will never see the true nature of my emotions. In order to go through with this, I need to put ice around my heart. And freeze it I do in that moment.

His lips take mine in a moment of domination and surrender, the dance of a woman and a man in full play. Lincoln's hands reach down, slipping beneath my suit jacket and covering both ass cheeks. He kneads them, spreads them, as his tongue invades my mouth. I give over control, let him take me where he wants us to go, as I fist my hands in those beautiful locks.

The kiss goes from a discovery, a searching exploration, to fucking with our mouths. It's hot and heavy; the bathroom suddenly feels like a sauna, and sweat slicks my skin.

Breaking off before this all moves too quickly, I slap a hand to the bare skin exposed by his undone buttons.

"No sex." I hold a finger up at him.

I see it, that flicker of disappointment at not being able to put his cock inside me. I'm not saying I'm not disappointed, but this is both a measure to protect myself and to coax him into coming back. If you make something off-limits to a man, or a football jock with the mentality of a ten-year-old, he'll crawl at your ankles until you give it to him.

"But that doesn't mean I can't do this."

He turns me so that I face the mirror, those gorgeous features watching every muscle of my expression. Slowly, he brings his hand up, caressing my cheek and then skimming down my neck. His fingers brush over my collarbone, and I swallow, realizing I'm absolutely parched. But before I can catch my breath, or try to swim above the hazy fog of lust settling firmly over my senses, Lincoln strikes.

That large, callused hand settles right over my heart, in between my breasts. He's touching my bare skin, so close to the nipples that could cut steel at this moment, watching my face as he undoes me. I can barely breathe, every inch of my flesh buzzing with arousal. If he cups my breast right now, I know my panties will flood with desire.

"You're a fucking knockout." He breathes in my ear, our eyes never breaking connection in the mirror.

I lean back into him as he slides his hand in, rolling a nipple between his thumb and forefinger. Shuddering, the sensation only serves to create more friction between my legs as I grind against Lincoln's tented pants. He's so hard, I can feel the pulse of the head of his cock beneath the material.

I want to unzip him, feel the hot weight of him in my hand. Because as much as I'm doing this to further my plan, to get revenge on Lincoln, I'm a woman. I have needs. I want to have fun and let loose in a bathroom at a party. These are supposed to be the wildest times of my life, and I'm ready for them.

Before I know what's happening, Lincoln's hand is passing the elastic of my underwear, moving down until it finds the wet, swollen nub between my thighs.

"Oh my God," I moan as he circles his forefinger around it, rubbing in the spot that makes me see stars.

"That's right, watch what I do to you." His deep vibrato echoes through my skin.

Lincoln watches me as his fingers invade me, as he works me higher and higher, my knees shaking. His other arm holds me around the waist to keep me from falling. His lips work my neck, my arms reaching back to grip onto those sexy, lumberjack locks.

I'm squirming, my climax building to a height it's never

reached before. The moment he pushes another finger inside me, I feel the wire snap, and with it, all of my control.

"Come on my fingers, Henley. I want to taste them hours after we leave here."

His shameless dirty talk throws me over the edge of the cliff, a brick tied to my ankles.

I come in puffs of breath, moaning into the air of the bathroom. Lincoln watches my face so intensely, it's like he's studying this portrait to paint it from memory. He doesn't remove his fingers as my orgasm coats them, the pressure of those thick digits only prolonging the shudders that wrack my body.

The high of my orgasm still sings through my muscles, but I know what I need to do. Not only do I want to feel him, to taste him on my tongue, but I need to leave Lincoln craving. A stellar blow job is just the way to keep him coming back for more.

I turn quickly, dropping to my knees before him and working his belt. He doesn't protest, doesn't say that I don't need to repay him. Yes, he's a scumbag from the rumors I've heard, but he's also a hot-blooded male who isn't going to turn down a chance to be sucked off. He's not the gentle, eager-to-please guy. He knows his power, his ego, and he brandishes them like a sword.

In seconds, I have him in my hand, the full, throbbing heat of him enormous on my palm. With an anaconda like this in his pants, no wonder he walks around campus like the whole world can see his cock.

"*Fuckkk* ..." Lincoln breathes as I deep throat him in one swallow.

Having no gag reflex really comes in handy when you're trying to seduce a known player and ruin his life.

I suck at him, pulling him into my mouth with just the right amount of suction. I let him grab my chin, tangle his fingers in my newly dyed hair, and curse obscenities above me every time I lick that certain spot just by his balls.

In a matter of minutes, I can feel his knees begin to shake, and the curses come more frequently.

"I'm going to come. Fuck, Henley, I'm going to ..."

Lincoln explodes down my throat; the salty taste not a welcome one, but I can bite back the initial disgust of it. No girl ever likes to swallow, and if they tell you otherwise, they're lying.

But I'm no coward, and when I set out to do a job, I finish it.

Every drop he gives me, I swallow, relishing his husky growls and the way his wild eyes come undone as he looks down at me. As I stand, the alcohol wearing off, I'm aware that I need a stiff drink to recover from this encounter.

Because Lincoln Kolb *is* as good as they say, and part of me wants to do this over and over again. Even in a dingy bathroom.

I notice the way he doesn't kiss me after I blow him, which is basically the equivalent of a fuckboy saying he doesn't want feelings involved.

Damn, that was *fun*. And as I grin at Lincoln in the mirror behind me, his thick fingers that smell of me running through those gorgeous brown locks, I take pride in the satisfied, exhausted smirk on his face.

I, once again, have him right where I want him.

I wipe the condensation from the mirror.

Every single one of my muscles ache, from the cords in my neck to the flexors in my ankles. We had a gym session today that could have kicked JJ Watt's ass, and I'm a guy who likes to pride himself on being in shape.

I know I said it before, but college is a whole different ball game. Or playing field. Or whatever sports metaphor you want to use to describe it as really fucking hard compared to high school. The trainers here are at the top of their game; they know which muscle to work to get you throwing better, running better, winning fucking championships.

But it doesn't come without full-body paralysis after, thus the forty minute, scalding hot shower I just took. At least it's the middle of the day, and everyone else is in classes. I've witnessed a few fights over the showers on my dorm floor, and I'm in no shape to kick someone's ass for bitching at me about using all the hot water.

As an athlete, my school schedule is a joke. I take the minimum amount of credits each semester so that it can look like I'm working toward graduating, even though I'm going to declare for the draft my junior year. My courses consist of education seminars that a monkey could pass, and I barely have to attend before the professor puts an A on my paper.

I'm a decently smart guy, memorizing entire playbooks isn't for dummies, and I could probably take on more challenging material. But I don't want to. The only thing I've ever wanted to do is play football and sidetracking from my dream will only mean both areas of my focus would suffer. So, I don't split them.

It's why I'm alone on the dorm floor while everyone is attending two p.m. classes. The football team is done with our second workout of the day, and I'm so fucking pumped for this weekend.

Our first game. I haven't been named the starter, but I'm hoping Coach Daniels will let me get a rep or two in. Over the past week and a half, I've been rotating in with the first team, and my numbers don't lie. I've hit pass after pass, aced every drill they asked me to. During our scrimmage the other day, I beat Wayne Tivan's passing yards by fifty, and that was with the B squad. Wayne is the junior starting quarterback who played for Warchester all season last year. He's decent, but he's not me.

Soon enough, I'll be leading the university's team to victory. For now, I just have to focus and keep my head on straight.

In the mirror, my scar gleams a bright, nasty red after being exposed to such hot water for such a long time. I run a finger down it, thanking God I haven't had to explain it to anyone just yet.

Especially Henley. That girl has no weakness, and the last thing I want is sympathy from the spitfire. I wouldn't be able to bear seeing pity in her eyes when she finds out I was the kid in elementary school with cancer. The one who missed six months of school for chemo, the one they had fundraisers for, the little boy whose shaved head appeared in his second grade yearbook.

She didn't get a glimpse of it, seeing as the only thing I could manage to get off my body was my pants and boxers before succumbing to Henley and her scarlet-haired seduction. Fuck, who knew that even without those blond curls to grab onto, I'd be so fucking attracted to her that I'd have to actively stop myself from blowing my load too soon.

Jesus Christ. Her mouth, those lips, the perfect suction she created. The way she almost growled my name as I added another finger inside her and made her come all over my hand. Just thinking about the way she tossed her head back, those light brown eyes rolling ...

It gets me hard as a steel pipe just thinking about it. I might need to get back in the shower to finish myself off, let the hot spray wash the come away.

This is the type of girl who could get me in trouble. Because we hooked up, we got all of that sexual chemistry out of our system. Even if I didn't lay her down and lay into her, I got my nut off and that was usually enough.

I'm beginning to realize that one time will never be enough with Henley Rowan.

We went at it in the bathroom at the CEOs and hoes party two days ago, and I haven't been able to stop thinking about it since. I want to track her down, drag her back to my dorm, but I know how desperate that looks. She barely talked to me after we left that bathroom and had the nerve to sidle up to some other dude at the flip cup table. Henley stayed at the party with her roommate for probably an hour or two after our hookup and never spoke to me or looked my way once.

Usually, I was the one to brush someone off after a hookup. I kind of felt used by her. And that feeling pissed me off, along with the fact that it gave her the upper hand again.

It might make me look clingy, finding her after she clearly wanted a one and done, but I know I won't be able to keep away from her.

There are bigger fish to fry, though. After my post-shower routine, I head back to my room, deck out in Warchester football sweats, and plop down on my bed with a protein bar.

Picking up my cell, I hit the speed dial for Mom's number.

"Honey! I miss you!" she screeches when she picks up the phone.

My mom is one of the kindest, most affectionate people to ever walk the earth. She's one of those moms who would have homemade snacks for us the minute we stepped off the school bus. My mom is the glue that holds our family together, both tough and also flowing; she can be the dictator when she wants, but gooey and lovey ninety percent of the time.

She and my dad created the perfect childhood for Chase and me, and now they were trying to do the same for my cousins.

"Hi, Ma, I miss you, too. You guys are coming to the game this weekend, right?"

Even though there was a small chance I'd play, my parents had already promised to bring Tyla and Brant to see me in uniform at Warchester for the first time. My little cousins were so excited, and my parents only matched their enthusiasm. Chase would be here, too, but his wife was eight months pregnant, and getting a flight from Chicago this close to the baby just wasn't possible.

"Wouldn't miss it for the world, buddy. How you feeling?" There is a clatter in the background, and I just know she's getting the snacks ready for my cousins to come from school to.

I miss home in the way you miss an old movie you really love. The nostalgia of it, the familiarity and routine that never changes. I mostly miss walking in the door and having those rug rats tackle me. They've had a tough life in their short years, and all of us are only looking to make it better.

"I'm fine, just ready to play. How are Tyla and Brant? How did the hearing go?" My voice is so anxious, I can't even hide it.

Mom takes a deep breath, because she knows how fired up I can get about all of this. "Lincoln, there really hasn't been much progress since we called two weeks ago—"

"Come on, Mom. Just tell me." I try to reason with her.

Before I left for school, Mom and Dad sat me down and told me that I didn't have to be invested in every second of the custody battle. That they wanted me to focus on having fun at college, at playing as well as I could. That they could handle all the legal issues with my cousins.

I know they can, but it doesn't mean I don't want updates by the second.

She sighs again, but I know she's going to tell me. "Aunt Cheryl was there this time. None of us expected her to show up, but apparently she could stay sober enough for a few hours to appear like a viable option for the children's parental guardian. Seeing as she hasn't shown up for months, and that Donny was in attendance, they didn't grant her anything further than one supervised visit a month. But it's going to be another two weeks until we can re-up our guardianship, so I am prepared for a fight."

Anger, so hot and blinding, hits me square in the chest. "They allowed her visitation with that fucking criminal sitting in the courtroom? They know his rap sheet!"

"Lincoln, watch your mouth," Mom warns, and then sighs. She does a lot of sighing these days. "And yes, they did. I have no idea why the legal system favors some of these parents, although it breaks my heart that Tyla and Brant can't have the love of their mother. But considering who she is, I want them with me. I just … I never thought she'd turn out this way."

Cheryl is her baby sister, the youngest of four, and has always had issues. From what Mom has told me, her sister got involved with drugs at a young age and just never stopped. It's been years of neglect, abuse at the hands of their mother and her boyfriends, and passing off to family members for Tyla and Brant. I wish Cheryl would just go away, just put the final nail in the coffin of her relationship with her kids. For their sake.

Now, the court-appointed year of guardianship my parents won is almost up. They wanted to adopt my cousins legally, to finally get them out of my aunt's care, but it's at this very moment she has decided to fight for them. It's all a farce, all for show or for manipulation, who really knows.

"They can't grant her her rights back," I say firmly.

"They shouldn't, but it isn't up to us. We just have to keep providing a loving home for Tyla and Brant, and hope that the law and the universe are on our side." Mom's voice is cautiously hopeful.

It's all we have—hope. And that can be a dangerous thing.

"Okay, obviously, you know this is the shutter button. And this is how you adjust the focus. I can teach you a little more about lighting on Photoshop later."

Jamie straightens my camera, coming up close to a group of wildflowers. We chose the arboretum on campus to shoot our first project for our Composition of Photography class, which we shared as well as Kyle's class, because of the easy canvas and beautiful landscape. Taking photos of flowers and plants wasn't as challenging as people, and it always provided for a pretty picture, no matter the lighting.

I was helping her, teaching her some of the photography basics, and she was turning out to be a natural. I didn't often let someone borrow my camera, but there was something about Jamie that I just trusted. Maybe it was because her soft-spoken sarcasm reminded me of Catherine, but I'd let her get her shots first. And then, I'd take some more difficult angles to really wow our professor. I might be helping Jamie, but I was here to show off what I could do.

The dye Rhiannon convinced me to go with is nearly out of my hair. There are just a few tips at the end still blazing with the fire of scarlet red, and I can't wait for them to leave. Because those scarlet tips keep reminding me of what I did the other night with Lincoln Kolb.

And how I can't stop thinking about it. How I can't stop thinking about how he knew the exact right way to make me come. Or the way his breathy grunts and curses filled my ears, made me feel like that Ariana Grande song, "*God is a Woman*."

I have to stop thinking about him like this. I have to let fury rule my brain, and my heart.

Now that the hair dye task is complete, I only have four more to go.

6. ~~Dye my hair~~
   7. Have sex
   8. Camp out in a tent
   9. Go bungee jumping
  10. Get revenge on Lincoln Kolb

Number seven goes right along with number ten, and although Catherine never cashed in her virginity card before she passed, I already have. So I guess I could cross that off, but I'll amend it to be sex with Lincoln, as I'm pretty sure she would have lost it to him if it hadn't been for her cancer recurrence.

How strange to think that Catherine would have been claiming the penis I touched in a bathroom on Saturday night. Sometimes, in all of this, I forget how much she was into him. She'd talked about dating Lincoln Kolb for ages before it happened, and while she was with him, it was like sunshine and rainbows every day.

I can still remember the look on her face when she told me he broke up with her. The bastard was going to get what was coming to him.

Aside from the two biggest ones left, I had camping and bungee jumping. Neither one of which I was looking forward to.

"All right, I think I got it. Can we take a snack break now?" Jamie whines.

"I'm in." I pick up my iced coffee, downing it in a satisfactory gulp from the straw. "God, why is coffee so good?"

"Nectar of the gods. Pairs perfectly with a sea salt chocolate chip." She hands me a cookie from her bag.

I take a bite and audibly groan. "Oh my God, did you make this?"

She nods. "Yep, whipped them up in the common room kitchen this morning."

"Jesus, this is what you need to be doing with your life." I point at the cookie, which is now almost half gone.

"Thanks, but it's so hard to get into pastry, or baking. Plus, everyone's goal in that industry is to like, own their own business or open up a shop. Or be a foodie Instagramer. It's so saturated."

I snort, motioning for her to pass me another. "And what do you think the photography industry is? Beautiful photography accounts on Instagram are like Starbucks in New York City. Spit and you'll hit one every time."

Jamie chuckles. "Yeah, I guess."

"I'm serious, though. I could start photographing some of your treats. Put them on IG. See what happens. It's dumb not to go for something you love. Believe me, life is too short."

My voice must take on some odd note, because she eyes me cautiously. "You okay?"

I shrug, emotion suddenly overcoming me. It's weird, grief. Some days, I'm fine. I can go hours without thinking of Catherine. And then other days, I cry if I get a whiff of what I think is the perfume she used to wear. Or when I'm looking at a certain color wall, and it reminds me of the time we splattered paint all over her bedroom to make it look edgy.

"My ... I lost someone close to me at the end of the school year, just before graduation. It's ... some days are better than others."

It feels good to tell someone, even if I don't specifically talk about Catherine. No one at Warchester knows what I'm dealing with under this tough exterior, and my chest heaves open in relief at admitting a small part of it to Jamie.

She touches my hand. "I'm so sorry. If you ever want to talk about it, I'm here."

It's a simple statement, a small show of camaraderie. But it makes a big difference. "Thanks."

"In the meantime, I have a walnut blondie recipe I've been wanting to try out. Want to come help me make it, maybe take a few free marketing photos for your portfolio?" She crosses her fingers.

"If I get to taste test, I'm in." I nod, smiling.

I may never find the friendship I had with Catherine, but it's turning out that there are other females out there who may understand me just as well.

Another Friday night in college, another party.

Only tonight, I'm not drinking. During season, we're not allowed to drink the night before games, and honestly, we really shouldn't be drinking the week before either. Saturday, after the game, is the only party night we're allowed. But no one is going to go running to coach if one of the players has a beer at the end of a long Tuesday.

I can't help it if I'm supposed to be here in support of the team, at the team house off campus, and there is a party going on. None of us are drinking, most of us are looking for a hot chick to hook up with to calm our nerves before game day, and parties just keep your mind off of stressful shit.

The place smells like sex and sweat, and I won't lie, I could go for a hot fuck right now.

Except, my dick is an asshole. Because the only girl he seems to want won't give him the time of day.

I can't take my attention off her. I've been keeping an eye on Henley all night. It's not a coincidence she keeps showing up to the parties she'll know I'll be at. If she didn't want to encounter me, she could go to another party, or try to sneak in underage at the bars. So I don't understand why she won't come over here, or why she's pretending not to see me smirk across the dance floor when our gazes collide.

We've not spoken or seen each other since the night in the bathroom, not that I haven't tried. I've gazed around the quad each time I've passed through, looking for her. I suppose I could have gone through some channels to get her number, but I didn't want to look too desperate.

The moment she makes a move, her red cup in hand, I know it's my time to strike.

I step up to the keg, where she's about to fill her cup.

"If you can fill that with no foam, I'll let you keep pretending you're not looking at me across the party. If not, you have to kiss me again."

Henley doesn't even flick those big brown eyes up at me. I'm glad her hair is back to its normal color, the blond of a dimming sunset. It's the color you look out for over the horizon, and I want it on my pillow, in my sheets.

"I'm sorry, who was watching who across the party?" I see the tilt of her lips through the curtain of her hair.

I step into her space, not caring that I'm the one desperately trying to pursue her. "Pour your beer, Jimmy."

"I can't with you distracting me, *Stallion*," she quips.

"Ah, so I do get under your skin. I wasn't sure I could weasel my way in there."

Banter is our foreplay, and I'm ready to get to the main attraction.

Henley's thumb presses the top of the tap, beer spilling from the faucet, and we both watch in anticipation. The cold, carbonated liquid fills her cup, and I want to tell her to go faster. It feels like time all but stops, because damn, I want the foamy head to appear on the top of that drink.

"Careful now, looks like you're tilting it too much," I tease, trying to make her mess up.

Henley's slim wrist rotates on her cup, pulling it up just a second too soon, and voilà, a foamy sea covering the top of her beer.

"Oh, damn. *You lose.* Guess you'll have to kiss me now." I pucker my lips.

"What if I wanted to lose?" she challenges, spite dancing in her eyes.

"Then I guess you have to kiss me, *babe*." I puff out my chest, a cocky grin stretching my lips.

Henley rolls her eyes. "I'm not your babe."

"What, you don't like that nickname?"

"I thought my nickname was Jimmy." She folds her arms, and I want to rip off the tiny white tank top she's wearing.

"And you know mine is Stallion."

Henley eyes me, and I can't read her expression. Without breaking our stare, she tips the cup to her lips and chugs, her long black eyelashes batting against her cheeks. She doesn't stop until the last drop is drank, and then tosses the cup aside.

And leans up on her toes to kiss me.

Right there, in front of the entire party, blocking the line to the keg, she slaps her hand around the back of my neck and claims my mouth. It's sexy and badass, the way she picked up my gauntlet and ran away with the prize. Because neither of us lost in this little bet ... oh hell no, no one's losing as she melts into me and I feel the blood rush to my cock.

Someone whistles, and I hear the catcalls begin.

"Come back to my room with me." I break away but keep my mouth on hers.

"You're drunk," she says.

"I haven't had a drop of alcohol. Are you drunk?"

"I had one beer." Her eyes flick up at me, assessing, searching.

"I'm not a gentleman, Henley. I want to fuck you so hard that you see stars. If you want that, which I know you do, come back to my room with me."

There is a distinct possibility she could say no. I'm half expecting her to turn me down, because she's shown no indication outside of that one hookup in the bathroom that she wants or needs me.

Maybe that's why I'm so drawn to her; I'm used to girls, both here and back in my hometown, pursuing me. I'm used to girls throwing themselves at me, I'm used to having the pick of the litter. That sounds fucking awful, but I've been an attractive athlete my whole life, I know that I have a draw. It's just the way things are, I didn't make up the rules.

But with Henley, I've finally encountered the hard-to-get girl everyone has always warned me about. The one who won't be impressed by me, or beg to fall into bed with me. Henley is elusive, mature, feisty and just downright confusing. Why is it that all men want the one woman that confuses them?

"Let's go. Before I change my mind."

I barely register her words before Henley is dragging me out of the party by the arm.

Wait a minute, she's going to come to my room?

Shit, I better bring my sexual A-plus game.

We barely talk on the way back to our conjoined tower buildings, mostly because I'm terrified I'll spook her.

I'm shocked when she turns to come into West tower with me, instead of brushing me off like the last time I walked her home from a party.

"If your sheets are dirty, I'm leaving." She chuckles, but we both know she's not joking.

It's a good thing I have a mother who taught me to do laundry. Well, *that* ... and that I haven't slept with someone since I got to Warchester. First, it was because of preseason, and then it was because I was trying to convince *this* girl to have sex with me.

By the time we reach my door and I swipe my ID to unlock it, my heart threatens to beat out of my chest.

Because this isn't just any girl, and that feels strange to me. I've been trying to get Henley alone for almost three weeks now, which for me is a long time. Sure, I had the odd high school girlfriend, which really didn't mean much. We'd hookup at parties or go to the movies or eat half-price appetizers at Applebee's on Friday night.

No, I hadn't been this determined about a girl in a long time, and even though we had no promises between us and this probably wasn't going anywhere, I was into her. For more than just her looks.

So, fuck, I really wanted this to go well. I know I have the moves on the mattress, I'm not doubting it. But what if Henley likes something I haven't tried on a girl yet? What if she's not into certain positions, or wants me to turn the fucking lights off. I hate it when girls want me to turn the lights off. Half the fun of fucking is seeing what I do to you when I do it.

"So, this is the ultimate bachelor cave." Henley walks around my room, her finger trailing over my dresser and desk.

I square my shoulders, ego firmly back in place. I know how to play her body like a damn guitar, and I suck at instruments. In the bathroom last weekend, I made her come harder than any girl I've ever had my fingers in. Fuck, was that sexy.

Walking up behind her, I sweep the curtain of blond curls aside to reveal her bare neck, nothing but a spaghetti strap covering her all the way down on her shoulder.

"That's right." My lips find the spot that made her shiver last weekend, and I lick it.

Sure enough, as if on cue, Henley quivers against me, her response making my dick spring to life. Slowly, I feast on her neck, hitting every citrus-scented spot I know makes her weak.

A small laugh comes from her throat as I make my way to her shoulder. "How are we going to fit in that bed together? How do you even sleep in that thing?"

She points to my bed, the same extra-long sized twin every college student gets issued in their dorm room.

I chuckle, because she has a point. "Part of me thinks they

make them that small so when we're getting busy, we have to get *real* close."

And without further ado, I spin her, pick her up, and deposit her so that she's sitting on my bed, legs spread open. Before Henley can blink, I move between them, taking her jaw in my hands and pulling her lips to mine.

My tongue glides into her mouth, kissing her furiously. I've been patient for too long, composed and confident for more than I can bear. Now that I have her here in my room, I'm going to let my control slip.

I focus in on her lips; the beauty mark right above them. Bending, I press my tongue to it, craving to taste every inch of her. Her hands pull at the hem of my T-shirt as she moans, my throat vibrating with the sound. Up and over my head it goes, and then her fingers are exploring every inch of my abs and chest, tangling in the patch of hair that dips below my belt.

Unfortunately, for me, but also fortunately, Henley doesn't whine about turning the lights off. That's because this woman is wholly secure in her beauty, as she should be. I can't wait to watch every curve of her body, as I go down on her, as I enter her ...

But it does mean she hesitates as her fingers run over my scar. The jagged, puckered skin on my stomach that makes me want to shrink back.

Instead of showing any vulnerability, I move faster, removing her top, unhooking her bra, so that her fantastic rack falls into my palms. They're perky and heavy, and I can't help but take her nipples in my mouth.

"Christ," Henley curses, and I smile against her skin.

"Not Christ, just Lincoln," I taunt, before pushing her back toward the pillows and climbing over her.

Henley rolls her eyes, but mid-roll I unbuckle my pants and shrug out of them, and when my cock springs free, she audibly gulps. She reaches for me, and as much as I want those slim little fingers pumping around me, I know I have to do something first. I *need* to do it.

I move down her body, my blood pounding in my ears. Henley is squirming on my sheets, and I can smell the musk of her before I even settle my mouth between her thighs.

And when I do.

Holy fucking hell.

I've never heard sounds like this from a girl. Or maybe I have, but they haven't made my heart drop and my cock tingle quite the way Henley seems to be able to. Her breathy little moans light a fire inside my chest, and as I feast on her, it only serves to turn me on more.

The scent of her, the way she's writhing against me and the bed, it's ecstasy. And I'm not even inside of her yet. The way she's so unashamed in her sexuality, of gripping my head and pulling me into her pussy as I eat it—I've never encountered a girl like this. It's fucking sexy, and right before I just know she'll explode on my tongue, I pull back.

"*Condom,*" she pants, her cheeks a pretty pink.

With the taste of her on my lips, I reach for my desk drawer beside my bed and strap up. The latex stretches down my cock, my fingers pinching the head, and then I'm positioned on top of her, Henley's legs spread and eyes glazed over with desire.

"Turn around. Show me that ass," I demand.

As much as I want to take this slow, to move in between her legs while she winds them around me, I've wanted to see that ass bounce as I wrap my fist in her hair even more.

She rolls, rising up on all fours, and goddamn it, if I died right now I'd be a happy man.

And then I push into her, both of our heads thrown back, and now I could *really* be at the pearly gates.

"You're the fucking sexiest thing I've ever seen," I growl in her ear, her ass jutting up against me.

Henley's back is bowed, so arched because of the way she's pressing against my cock and my hand controls her hair that she's the picture of ecstasy. The exact Coke bottle shape I've fantasized about since I had my first wet dream, I wish I could take a picture of this to revert back to when she inevitably leaves.

"Fuck me." She turns her head, those brilliant eyes daring me to drill her to kingdom come.

So I do. I grip her hips and thrust so hard and so fast that I think I'm going to render myself blind and deaf by the time this is over. If anyone was sleeping on this dorm floor, they surely aren't now. Between her near screams and my shouted dirty talk, we're quite a pair.

It's as if my cock was made to fit her pussy; we were created to dismantle each other on this fucking twin bed we're about to break.

"Don't stop, don't stop, don't stop," Henley mutters helplessly before letting out a careening wail.

Her head sinks into the pillow, her ass jutting up and changing the angle of my thrusts as she comes and squeezes around my dick. I come with a haggard breath as my vision goes white.

And by the time the last shutter leaves my body, I am sure I want to do this all over again.

W hen I finally see him in the dim lamp light, after we finish, it's as if my breath has been stolen right out of my lungs.

The system that helps me draw life is failing, simply because this man is so freaking perfect, his gorgeous body requires all the oxygen in the room.

Lincoln is like a Disney prince, all popping muscle and perfectly flowing hair. He's a demi-god, on the level of Hercules. This is the type of body you see in that issue of *ESPN Magazine*, or on display as a statue in the most famous art museums in the world. I want to memorize every chiseled dip, the mussed up sexiness of his mocha-colored hair. The stunning, taunting chromatic twinkle of his eyes.

And yet, there is one flaw. One long, wide, gashing scar slicing through the left side of his abs. It's rippled and cuts off the set of eight carved muscles that Lincoln boasts. The skin there is puckered, and a slight pinkish hue as opposed to the golden tan of the rest of his skin. It looks like someone took a machete knife and tried to serve him as the Thanksgiving day bird.

My fingers go to it without thinking. "How did this happen?"

Lincoln sucks in a breath as I trace the one blemish of his immaculate form. "Football."

There is something strange about his tone, and I realize he's lying. Wherever he got this, it wasn't from the sport he loves.

Lincoln is staring at me, I can feel it, and my cheeks heat. "What?"

I didn't mean to sound so insecure, but I almost want to cover my face before meeting his eyes.

"You're gorgeous, you know that, right?" He searches my face.

We already had sex, so why is he saying that? Lincoln doesn't strike me as the errant compliment kind of guy, and I already let him put his penis inside me, so what is going on?

And *my God*, my cheeks heat again just thinking about what we just did. That was, hands down, the best sex I've ever had.

I hadn't meant to sleep with him this soon. I was going to wait until our third encounter, like the dating rulebook says. Or maybe I could have held off and scored a nice dinner out of it ... a rarity for a college girl. But there was something in Lincoln's body language tonight, some kind of desperation that I could sense.

If I went back to his room tonight, he wouldn't be able to not see me again. I'm not sure how I knew this, but from the way he couldn't keep his eyes off me at that party, to the soberness of his plea, I knew I'm going to hook him tonight.

I swear, the look in his eyes when we first walked in here was ... nervous. I think that for just one second, the brash, confident demeanor I'd been putting on scared *the* Lincoln Kolb. For one vulnerable second, he wasn't the big man on campus. It's how I know I'm breaking him down.

And just like that, I've also crossed off another thing on Catherine's bucket list. It feels weird, thinking about her while

I'm naked and pressed up against Lincoln. I wonder, if she was alive, how she would have gotten revenge on him.

But I can't think about her now, or I'll have a mental breakdown.

"Thanks." I shrug, fully aware that we're snuggling because we can't not in this bed.

It's that awkward point in the night, the thing that happens after all the lust dissipates. You're stuck lying in a bed with a virtual stranger, who just put his most private body part in your most private body part, wondering how you should leave. Or, if he wants you to stay and if you want that, too.

I glance over at the clock on his bedside table, and it says one a.m. Not terribly late, there will still be plenty of drunk people stumbling back up to the dorms. Plus, I don't even have to walk outside, considering the two towers are connected on the second floor by a cafeteria. But this hookup wasn't just about sleeping with Lincoln, driving him insane.

It's about keeping him. Securing his attention, making sure his focus is pinned on me. He usually scoots girls out the door the minute he's done coming and never thinks about them again. If I sleep here, leave my scent on his pillow and my pussy tattooed on his brain, I'll be one step closer to my goal.

Getting him to fall in love with me.

So that I can then destroy his heart.

"Should I? I can ... um ..." I trail off, mostly because I'm as conflicted as he looks.

If I admit I want to stay, it makes me look attached. Which I want to be, but I want him to be the one to suggest it. If I go, I run the risk of Lincoln thinking this is a casual thing. It also could serve in me playing more hard to get, which might be a good outcome. This whole fucked-up game is like a chess match. One wrong move and he'll be yelling checkmate.

"Stay." He plants a hand on my hip. "I should be ready to go again in another five."

This makes me snort in surprise. "I wasn't aware there would be a second showing tonight."

Lincoln slaps a hand to his perfectly sculpted chest. "Offense taken. I'm a quarterback, I throw touchdowns all night long, baby."

"You really are a cocky bastard, aren't you?" I chuckle.

His roommate must be another football player, because there is nothing in this room other than Warchester football paraphernalia and a ton of food. Lincoln isn't messy, per se, but this is a typical guy's room. Sports stuff everywhere, clothes thrown on top of the dresser and not in the drawer. His shower stuff isn't contained in his caddy and there are protein bar wrappers everywhere.

"You know it. Let me show you just how cocky I can be." He rolls over on top of me, his stiffness pressed against my leg before he leans down to kiss me again.

A flash flood of guilt sloshes around in my stomach. This is horrible, what I'm doing. What kind of person does this? Not only does sleeping with someone I don't like just to get something make me feel like a whore, but I'm planning to make this guy fall in love with me. So I can break his heart. That's so fucked up. If I ever read a story like this in the back tell-all section of one of those popular beauty magazines, I'd think the girl was a raging bitch.

But I can't think about that. I push it all out of my head, compartmentalize the hell out of my issues that surely would throw a therapist for a loop.

I made a promise, and I won't go back on it.

W*hy the hell am I at a football game?*

I keep asking myself this question over and over again, as if my mind is suddenly going to wake up from its temporary insanity.

I hate the sport, never liked it even when friends would drag me under those Friday night lights in high school. Men banging into each other, breaking their body parts, sweating and grunting, and I just don't get it, personally.

Although, I brought my EOS-1D X Mark II, one of my favorite DSLRs to shoot sports in. Not that I shoot them often, but once in a while the newspaper back in Little Port would be looking for someone to shoot a tournament, and I'd swoop in to take that day's money with ease. I shot all kinds of jobs for local groups, media outlets, and photo studios. I was better than good; they knew it, and would take less money than a professional adult photographer so I could fill my portfolio.

Why I have it with me now is beyond me? Because apparently, my number one goal is to shoot brain-dead jocks while they fly through the air. I shoot a test shot from my seat, and have to admit, the photo I just captured of one player leaping into the air to catch the ball during warmups is pretty spectacular.

It only felt like minutes later when the dawn light poured through the half-drawn shades in Lincoln's room this morning. I guess that's what I get for staying up and having sex with him two more times. When I woke, it was to him pressing a kiss to my cheek, which is surprisingly intimate. Like something a couple who has been dating for a year or two would do. And then he'd asked if I'd come to his game tonight, and I couldn't not jump at the chance to get him closer to my spider web.

So here I am, at a college football game seeming to lust after a guy I secretly loathe more than anything else on earth.

"I can never figure out what to eat at these things." Rhiannon looks genuinely frustrated.

I chuckle, feeling bad I dragged her here. "What do you mean?"

"Well, it's like, I want to get popcorn. But then I know in the next quarter I'll want cotton candy, so I have to get that, too. And then by the time the last ten minutes comes around, you feel like a good ice cream, ya know? Sports games are just so tough to attend because there is too much food in too little time."

I tap a finger to my chin. "Aren't there different periods to this thing?"

She fingers a lock of pink hair. "Um, you don't even know that there are quarters in football, yet here we are dick chasing? I underestimated you, Henley. You're a hussy."

My roommate has a whip of a tongue that I truly appreciate. "I never said I knew anything about sports. I'm a creative, sue me."

"So am I, sort of, but it doesn't mean I've been living under a rock. Okay, I guess that was harsh. My dad represented a lot of football players, he's a money manager, and being his only kid, a daughter, meant I had to endure countless football Sundays. Do you want me to teach you the rules?"

I shake my head. "Not one bit. I'm here to watch and be clueless and maybe get a few cool shots."

She smiles. "Got it. And here to ogle the dude you went home with last night."

"Maybe that, too," I confess, my heart kicking up a notch.

"He's smokin'. Good pick. I did a little cheer when you texted me you were in his room. Is he a freak? Does he have a big dick?" she inquires, completely serious about her questions.

Two sets of parents in the bleacher row in front of us turn to give Rhiannon stern looks. My God, I hope those aren't Lincoln's parents. That would be just my luck.

My hand covers my mouth as I snicker at my roommate's loose lips. "Can we maybe talk about this later?"

"What? As if these people have never had a one-night stand." She rolls her eyes and cups her hands over her mouth. "Y'all know you banged it out in your dorms back in the day, don't judge us millennials for getting it in."

I wrap an arm around her neck and pull her head down to my shoulder to shut her up. My cheeks flame with embarrassment as Rhiannon chuckles with glee.

When I let her up, she doesn't look the least bit remorseful or ashamed. *Man*, she has an ego made of Teflon. "I'm going to start my pre-game off with a soft pretzel. You want anything?"

"A Coke, please." I hand her a few bucks and she walks off.

I need something to settle my stomach, or at least pretend that soda is the thing making the butterflies flap their wings into its lining.

Because I refuse to acknowledge that a crush is starting to bloom in my chest for Lincoln Kolb. I knew going in that feelings and emotions would be tricky. Separating those kinds of things is difficult for us girls, no matter how badass we pretend to be. Even though I hate him, I want revenge for my best friend. It's challenging not to smile when I think of his cliché sex jokes. Being intimate with someone, no matter how much you despise them, changes your demeanor toward them. Especially when they're as charming as Lincoln Kolb.

And those freaking pants. Who the hell knew that football came with such scintillating uniforms? I shouldn't be warming to Lincoln, but I can't stop staring at his ass and the way his biceps fill out that jersey. It's also creepy the way I can tell him apart from everyone else, by the way the team seems to pulse around him.

Every so often, someone comes over to Lincoln to talk close in his ear, or consult an iPad. They all seem to gravitate toward him, even the coaches. He's wearing a soft baseball hat with Warchester's logo and not a helmet, and I know from before that Rhiannon told me he wouldn't be starting in the quarterback position for this game. She went on some long-winded rant about how he should be starting, but they like to ground newbies by making them watch from the sidelines for a while. Learn their place. As if Lincoln Kolb has ever had to learn his place in life.

He looks into the stands, searching. I don't even know how he knows I'm here, but as I watch the eyes that I can't seem to stop daydreaming about scan the crowd for me, I know that he does.

We both knew my coming today was a toss-up. He asked, and I hadn't responded. But I needed to draw him in. I needed to show a smidge of interest before the next phase of my plan. Which was pulling away completely.

I sit up straight, unmoving, waiting for his predatory glance to land on its prey. That's what I am to him, prey. He thinks he has the upper hand here, that he's controlling the narrative. Oh, how terribly sad for his lizard boy brain.

When our eyes connect, the right corner of his lips tug up, and he raises a brow. I give him the smallest of shrugs, and something silent passes between us. We've only spent one night together, and yet there is this connection. Maybe this is what Catherine was talking about whenever she mooned over him.

Which is more dangerous: the game I'm playing to break his heart, or the fact that mine is disappointed I'll have to ignore him in the coming days?

The fact that it's this attached already can't be a good omen.

"Linc!"

Tyla comes running into my arms, her tight black curls bouncing all over her head as she sprints across the football field.

I catch her, spinning her around by her armpits as she squeals.

"How is my favorite girl?" I nuzzle her cheek with my nose.

"I colored Peppa Pig and then I got ice cream, and we saw you on the field!" Her brain moves a mile a minute, and I love trying to keep up with the random thoughts that fly from her mouth.

"That's awesome, what flavor?" I ask.

"Vanilla and chocolate swirl with extra sprinkles!" She's so excited that she almost hits me in the face as I hold her.

"Good game, buddy." Mom comes up, kissing me on the cheek as she takes Tyla from my arms.

I high five Brant, because eight-year-old boys are far too cool for hugs. "Dude, it'll be you out here someday."

He and I talk a lot about his goals for football. I know he looks up to me, that he wants to follow in my footsteps, and I keep it in mind whenever I'm out here or in practice. There is a chance he's always watching or learning, and I never want him to have the wrong way set for him.

"Nice opening drive in the fourth quarter." Dad claps me on the back.

"Thanks." I nod, trying not to smile too much.

It's not humble to brag, especially not as a quarterback. Quarterbacks are supposed to be the level-headed leaders of a team, the guys who work their tails off and make sure everyone else looks good, but don't take any credit for it.

"I can't believe they let you play today! I was so happy we got to see it, because I didn't think we'd be able to," Mom gushes.

I didn't think they'd be seeing me play today either. The coaches have been adamant that I'm not the starter this season; some stupid made-up rule about grounding a hotshot like me to make me work harder for it. I get the whole "earn your keep" thing, but *come on*. I came in during the fourth quarter because we were down by three touchdowns and I nearly won the game. A few more minutes on the clock and I would have helped score that third touchdown. As it was, I helped our team grab two of the ones we needed to make up.

"I'm just hoping I get to keep playing." My tone is serious.

"You will. It'll come, the starting position, the glory. For now, just keep your nose to the grindstone and learn as much as you possibly can," Dad instructs.

That's my father, always a hard worker, and always one to instill those kinds of values in his kids. My parents are two of the most hardworking people I know, and they gave Chase and me everything we could have wanted, plus, the life lessons to go with them. What they're taking on with Tyla and Brant is no small feat; heading into their wind down years with two little kids that will need a decade or more of care, they're freaking saints.

As my family chatters on around me, a flash of sunset golden curls catches my attention.

Henley is making her way down the stadium bleachers, and I can see her easily from my position on the field. She's wrapped in a short-sleeve blue sundress, and goddamn does it make her look like the girl next door. When, in fact, I know she's quite the opposite.

Our gazes had caught before the game, and they do so now. She's watching me track her.

I don't miss the way Henley watches me with my family. Her cheeks sport a nice blush, one I'd like to see as I do wicked things to her with my mouth and fingers. There are questions in her expression as I hold Tyla on my hip, and I want to know what she sees when she looks at me like this.

Just as quickly, she walks off. Part of me wishes she'd come over here, but how am I going to explain that one to my parents? *Oh, this is the girl I fucked three times last night and damn was she incredible.* Yeah, I think not.

"Linc? Can we go grab pizza before we head home?" Dad asks in a tone that means he definitely already asked once.

I shake my head to clear it. "Yeah, of course. But only if we get Hawaiian."

"That's my favorite!" Brant's smile is so wide, I can't help but crack a smile of my own.

"I know it is. Let's do it." I suggested that type of pie because I know he loves it.

And these kids still have a hard time asking for simple things they want, because they're so used to being denied or yelled at for being children. My little cousins deserve everything they want out of life, and if that means pineapple on pizza, then I'll suffer through that.

An hour later, the five of us have demolished three pies,

Brant is playing on Mom's phone, and Tyla is nearly asleep in Dad's lap.

"Any other news on the adoption front?" I lower my voice so that the kids don't hear.

Dad shakes his head. "We don't have another hearing for a month, but I have to submit the application for another six months of temporary guardianship this week. And then in two weeks, Cheryl gets her first supervised visit."

"I'm so nervous I could just be sick." Mom rubs her chin, her eyes darting around.

I lay a hand over hers. "It's going to be fine. If it's supervised, there is nothing that could happen."

I don't say what we're all really thinking. Of course, a million things could go wrong. She could not show up and completely disappoint the kids. She could take them somewhere, or ditch the supervision. She could say something to them to upset them, or ... the list goes on and on.

"Enough about this, though. How else is school going? Are your classes going well? Any girls we should know about?" Mom asks, because she can't help herself.

She doesn't actually care if classes are going well, but I guess she does. But not in this instance. No, the whole point of her line of questioning was to ask if I have a girlfriend yet.

"Jeanie, leave the boy alone. He's playing the field," Dad answers for me.

I snort, because they're both so old fashioned about the whole thing.

"Not playing the field, and no girlfriend," I tell them without elaborating.

Because that's not quite the truth, is it? I'm not playing the field, but I'm not dating. However, there was a girl in my room this morning that I was pleasantly surprised waking up to, and one I'd like to see again. That's a big step, even if it's small, for me. I'm typically not into repeat performances, but I just can't get her out of my head.

And now that I have Henley's number, I made her give it to me before she scurried from my room, I could text her and ask her to celebrate my victory.

Technically, the team didn't win, but I did seeing as how they let me play a quarter.

And I feel like celebrating with her naked body in my bed.

It's been a full five days since I watched Lincoln score a touchdown in his first college game, and I've successfully avoided him since that moment.

See, I have to play the game. Guys my age don't want a solid, committed, dependable girl. They don't want a steady relationship, one that you can count on to remain steadfast without texting the other person five times every second.

No, guys between the age of seventeen to twenty-four want drama and strife when it comes to sex and love. They want unpredictable ups and downs, a roller coaster of emotions and make up fucking. I'm convinced they want girls my age to be what they deem "crazy" because it makes it more fun for them.

So, I'm being unreadable. The more I play hard to get, the more Lincoln is going to be drawn to me. We had mind-blowing sex and then I didn't call him. I didn't text him, or try to message him on social media. Although I saw him all over mine. Liking my photography pictures on Instagram, even sliding into my DMs.

I haven't responded to a single one. This is part of the plan, though I didn't realize that my vagina would be so sorely disappointed about it. Once you feed the beast, it's hard to go back. It had been a while since I'd had sex, and Lincoln gave it *good* food. Now, I want seconds, and I can't have them.

And then there is that intriguing scene I saw after the game. Lincoln with his parents, I know what they look like after Catherine made me social media stalk the guy for most of senior year. But who were those little kids hanging all over him? They were adorable, and seemed to worship him, which only serves to make him look like more of the golden boy that he is. They couldn't be his kids ... could they?

No way, I laugh the idea off. There has to be another explanation. One I want to get, and I'm kicking myself about the self-imposed blackout on Lincoln.

Another wave of guilt hits me unexpectedly, which seems to be happening a lot these days. I am not the type of girl who does something like this, but maybe this is what happens when your best friend dies. They say grief manifests itself in various ways, and maybe mine is turning into a vindictive bitch.

Seducing someone only to break up with them seems so cruel, though I understand why Catherine put this on her list. She was humiliated.

The hardest thing to cope with is that Lincoln seems *nice*. Sure, he's cocky and he's got that attitude that a person who has always been on top of the popular pyramid sports, but he's ... well, he acts like a good person. He's never disrespected me or given me the impression that he's rude or pushy with girls. He actually has a personality and can hold a conversation, unlike a lot of guys my age.

It's not for the first time, in the silence of my own room, that I wonder whether Catherine was only seeing one side of her breakup with Lincoln. Were her emotions so clouded by her diagnosis that she took his rejection as a bigger deal than it was?

And that makes me feel even more guilty, that I'm choosing

the side of the guy I'm sleeping with over my dead best friend. Catherine always put me first, even if I was wrong, and I should be doing the same.

My textbook on famous photographers lays open on my bed when my cell phone ringing distracts me. I wasn't really studying anyway, what with my fifth episode of *One Tree Hill* on "in the background."

"Hey, Mama," I say when I pick up smiling.

I miss my parents, which is something I didn't think I'd do being here. It's just the three of us, our little family unit, and we've always been close. But they raised me to be an independent spirit, and I've never leaned on them for much. So being homesick threw me for a loop, although Mom calls every day to try to bridge that gap.

"Hey, pumpkin. How you doing? Saw your latest Instagram post, that botanical garden on campus is just beautiful."

Mom is one of those parents who stalks their child's social media. She will constantly text me or DM me about my posts, about my high school classmates posts, and she recently started following Rhiannon, so she's got a mouthful to say about my roommate.

"Thanks, there was great lighting that day." I nod, though she can't see me.

"And Rhiannon's latest find with that band at the dive bar near campus? I very much enjoyed that!" My mom snaps her fingers on the other end, and I roll my eyes.

She's trying to be "hip" to impress Rhiannon, though my roommate is anything but the cold-shoulder kind of girl everyone would assume she is by her appearance. As I've found out, Rhiannon is willing to help anyone or give a lesson on anything she's passionate about.

"Yeah, she has a real ear for it. How's everything there?"

Mom makes a happy little chirp noise. "Just the same as

always. We're missing you. Dad and I tried the new Indian place the other night, it was pretty good. Trying to stop by Michaela's at least once a week and see how she's doing."

Her mention of Catherine's mom's name has my stomach dropping to my feet. I haven't talked out loud with anyone about Catherine since I left my hometown, and it was kind of a nice break not to have the shadow hanging over me on campus.

"How's she doing?" I try to keep my voice from trembling when I ask.

"Oh, sweetheart, she's not doing well. It's still so raw, as I'm sure you know. We all know. It's going to take time."

"Yeah." My voice cracks, betraying the tears I'm barely holding in.

It's tough to think about Catherine on my own, but talking to people who knew her? Jeez, it's like flaying my skin opening and pouring salt in the wounds.

"It's okay to miss her. To think about her." My mom's calming voice comes through the other end of the phone.

And that's when I lose it. I drop the phone, my hands coming up to my eyes. I sob, a silent, gut-wrenching wail that robs me of breath and sight. It's not fair, at all, that I'm sitting here and she's not. How is this even allowed? The world should be ashamed of itself. I'm ashamed of it.

Wiping my eyes and trying to gulp in a few breaths, I pick the phone back up.

"Sorry," I mutter through watery breaths.

"Oh, honey, you never have to apologize. Your love for her is still here, as is hers for you. She'd be so proud that you're strong, that you decided to head off to college."

"I know that," I say, even though it sounds false to my ears.

"Honey, anytime you need to vent or cry, you know you can always call me. I love you."

"I love you, too, Mom. I'm going to go, okay?"

"Okay. Say hi to Rhiannon for me." She sounds like she's trying to be hopeful.

I hang up, and my entire mood has dimmed.

I need to get out of this dorm room. It feels like it's suffocating me, like I'm in the grave with Catherine and I'll never get out. I know I should talk to someone about this, how there are moments during the week where I feel like I can't continue to breathe, like it's all sucked out and my vision sparks with dots. But that would lead to admitting what I'm doing to Lincoln, and I can't reveal that.

Grabbing my laptop, a few books, and my AirPods, I head out to the quad. Nothing a little sunshine and Photoshop can't fix. Hopefully.

I'm knee-deep in editing a series of photos of Rhiannon, I made her do a photoshoot two days ago, when someone calls my name.

I look up to see one of my classmates crossing the grassy sections of the quad, holding up his hand in greeting.

Alden is in a few of my photography classes, and while we don't gravitate toward the same subjects, his work is magnificent. He grew up in Queens and specializes in street photography. His portfolio is gritty, raw black-and-whites of the real life and struggle of some of New York City's most disenfranchised. It's mesmerizing to study, and he ain't bad on the eyes either. If Idris Elba had a younger brother, it would be Alden.

"Hey, baby girl, what you up to?" He fist bumps me and then plops down on my bench.

He's sitting close, and I get the feeling that his charm is the kind that can't be contained. From the moment I met him, he's been that enigmatic force that everyone seems drawn too. His smooth charisma and easygoing personality make him a fast friend, and someone that everyone wants to be around. It strikes me that I should introduce him to Rhiannon.

"Trying to work on some lighting on this one." I point to my laptop, where I have a picture of none other than my roommate up in Photoshop.

"Beautiful shot. Beautiful girl." He gets a closer look, leaning into me, his delicious cologne pricking my nose.

She is, obviously. But these pictures are some of my best work. I sent an early test shot to Kyle, my professor, and he had nothing but a great review for it. It's kismet that he just so happens to be my advisor, because he's laid out some great plans for my future both here and in photography. He even uttered the words *Time Magazine* the other day, and I almost collapsed on the floor.

"My roommate, Rhiannon. She's a riot, I have a feeling you'd like her. But I just can't get the lighting on the apples of her cheeks right—"

"Henley!" Someone barks, and both mine and Alden's heads shoot up.

I see Lincoln Kolb stalking across the quad. His eyes, one green, one blue, flit between Alden and I, our proximity. And I know that look, the fury barely contained. That man is jealous, green-eyed monster jealous.

My inner-schemer smirks smugly with pride. I'm slowly slipping under his skin, and my plan is going exactly according to how I want it.

"Lincoln, hey," I say easily, and Alden doesn't move from where he's examining Rhiannon on my laptop screen.

In fact, his thick hand is resting on my thigh because of how he's trying to help me adjust the exposure, and I don't miss the flash of annoyance that passes through Lincoln's expression.

"You haven't texted me back." He all but growls.

"Well, hi to you, too." I shrug. "Been busy."

The agitation pouring off of him is palpable. "No, you haven't. I saw you show up to my game."

"That was five days ago. I couldn't have been busy for the last five days?" I'm being a smart-ass and he's getting more and more pissed off about it.

After my breakdown about Catherine, I'm almost reveling shoving his face in this. He was one of the people who hurt her most, so the fact that I can anger him now has power simmering in my veins.

His head tips toward Alden. "Can we talk in private?"

Alden finally catches on that he's the third wheel here, although I kind of want him to keep his hand on my thigh. The shade of Lincoln's cheeks right now is giving me a sick pleasure.

"I'm gonna go." Alden begins to stand, and I smile at him, giving him a squeeze on the arm.

"Stop being such a chick, Lincoln. I'm working," I tell him, acting completely unaffected.

Lincoln watches Alden go, a threatening gleam in his eye.

"Didn't realize you were seeing someone." It's such a reach, and we both know he's only asking because he's pissed at Alden's hand on me.

"I'm not." I don't elaborate, and focus my eyes on my laptop.

"I'm sorry, did I do something wrong?" His tone changes, and I swear I hear hurt in it.

"Aside from storming up on me on the quad and insinuating I'm dating someone, no." I chuckle sardonically.

Lincoln sits down next to me, and it's so hard to resist the urge to look at him. Even if I haven't been responding to his texts or social media outreach, it doesn't mean I haven't been combing through his pictures, stalking like every millennial knows how to do. Those shirtless ab pictures on his Instagram are shameless, but it doesn't make them any less *hot*.

"I thought we had a good time the other night, Henley. A couple good times, if I remember. I thought we could do it again." He's ducked his head, trying to get me to look at him.

With him this close, I can smell the pure soap and tooth-paste scent of him. I want to have more good times, too, but I need to be unreadable.

After focusing on my laptop for another few beats, leaving him hanging, I finally glance up as if I haven't heard what he said.

"Yeah, sure. Send me a text sometime. I kind of have to finish this ..."

Lincoln looks a little crushed. Part of me feels like a total bitch, but then I remember how he dumped Catherine, and I mentally puff out my chest. This jerk deserves this, I have to keep telling myself that. I reach into my bag, rubbing the edge of the worn paper with Catherine's bucket list on it.

He rises from the bench, stutters as if he might say some-thing, and then walks off with a straight-legged, frustrated pace in the other direction.

Phase one of crushing the cocky jock, *completed*.

LINCOLN

The weights slam down on either side of my legs, and I huff out a violent breath.

"Jesus, dude, you're a *beast* today." Janssen claps his hands, the sound echoing around the weight room.

I breathe out of my nose in labored puffs, and I feel like I could breathe fire right about now. "What the fuck is wrong with chicks anyway?"

It comes out unexpectedly, but I'm so fucking angry about my interaction with Henley before that I can't help the outburst.

A couple of the guys around the weight room chuckle, and Derrick answers. "How much time do you have?"

"My girlfriend is on her period, so I feel you, brother." Christian, one of our defensive linemen, nods sagely. "Not that there is anything gross about it, we still have sex, but she's so fucking unpredictable; I don't know if I should rub her feet or leave a fifty-feet barrier between us at all time."

"Well, I'm messing around with this girl Jamie, and it's great because she brings me cookies and brownies before we have sex. So it's *all* fantastic," Janssen brags, and we all shoot him a death glare.

"Fuck you, bro." I throw a sweaty towel at his head.

"I feel like you can never understand what they want." Derrick nods his agreement, ignoring our bragging friend.

"You know what they say." Christian motions with his arms.

There is a beat, and we all lean forward as if he's going to impart some crucial wisdom.

"Men are from Mercury, women are from Venus." He nods like he's fucking Yoda.

Janssen cracks up. "Dude, it's men are from *Mars*, you dumbass."

"Nah, pretty sure it's Mercury." Christian's lips form into a confident grin.

"Aren't Mercury and Venus closer together than it is with Mars, so it wouldn't make sense? I think that's why the saying is Mars—" Derrick enters the debate, but I cut him off.

"Who the fuck cares? All I'm saying is, why do girls act like they're completely into you, come back to your room, let you dick them down three times and you even let them stay over, and then they ghost you?" I let out an exasperated grunt.

I wish I could punch the fucking wall in here, but I'd break my goddamn throwing hand and that would be good for no one. As it is, I'm pushing it too hard on the weights.

I've been in here for an hour, pushing my body to its physical limits, after I saw Henley getting pawed up by some other dude. It doesn't help that the guy looks jacked and suave and had his hand on her fucking thigh.

Why am I getting so worked up over this? We had sex once. Okay, we had sex three times, but only spent one night together. And then she came to my football game and clearly was only there to see me. I thought we were cool, that we could have some more fun, but apparently she has other plans.

"Dude, are you going crazy? Who is this about?" Janssen swigs from his water bottle, his eyebrows knitting in concern.

"Oh, shit, is this about that bangin' blond from the party the other night?" Derrick's eyes go wide.

I shrug, defeated, as I plop down on the weight bench next to me. "Yeah."

"And you care about this because ... ?" Derrick looks at me like I have two heads.

"I don't know, man, she's cool. And sexy as hell."

"You got that right," Janssen agrees. "The legs on her—"

"Hey," I cut him off, sending another death glare. "But you're right. They're some damn great legs. And I want to see them again. Problem is, she's gone radio silent on me. And then I just saw her in the quad with some other guy cozied up next to her."

"Maybe you didn't make her come," Christian deadpans, completely serious.

The other guys snicker while I flip him the bird. "I made her come. There is no doubt about that."

"You never know. Girls these days are masters at faking it," Derrick says.

"If you can't tell whether a girl actually came, or was just faking it, you're not a real man." Janssen puffs out his chest. "There is that gripping thing their pussy does when—"

I hold my hand up, not needing vivid detail of how my best friend satisfies women. "Bro, trust me, I'm good. I know I made her come, multiple times. It's not that."

"Then what do you think it is? Is that guy her boyfriend? Did she cheat?" Janssen asks.

The way said guy got up, as if he felt like an awkward third wheel while Henley and I minced words, there is no way he's her boyfriend. But it doesn't mean she isn't hooking up with anyone else, which I hadn't considered a possibility. The thought makes my stomach churn. We're nothing to each other than two people who shared some really great sex, but it feels like a little more. We have nicknames for each other, and a banter that is rare to find with another person. I thought we were onto something, and I'm just disappointed that she's completely ignoring my attempts to get in touch.

"No, she doesn't have a boyfriend. And I thought we had fun, hell, I'm *Lincoln Kolb*." I say this, sitting up a little straighter and trying to get my dick to commit to my ego.

"Maybe that's the problem. What if she's not into the whole 'macho football player' thing?" Christian asks.

I hadn't considered this. I've been so concerned coming into college that girls would get too attached to my persona, that they'd want me because of my status on the team and the fame I could maybe give them one day. I had never thought I'd meet a girl who seemed interested, and then got to know me, or my lifestyle, a little more and be turned off by it. But Henley had come to my game. Maybe she didn't like what she saw when it came to football. Maybe she didn't like what she saw in me that night in my dorm room.

Rubbing my chin, I nod. "Maybe. But if that's so, how do I get her interested again? And it's just plain rude not to answer texts. Or DMs."

"You texted her, multiple times? Without her answering? And *then* DMed her? Damn, dude, that looks so desperate." Janssen snorts.

"How many times have you ghosted a chick? Come on, Kolb, we all do it." Derrick smiles smugly, and I want to punch him because he's right.

"You gotta find out where her dorm room is. Maybe leave flowers. Or chocolate." Someone pipes up from the corner, and I notice the entire weight room is in on our conversation.

"Or a chicken, bacon, ranch pizza from that place in Collegetown. That's the way to my girlfriend's heart." Christian walks over to the bench press and starts setting it up.

"I think that's too aggressive," I say, doubting their advice.

"Or romantic. Depends on which way you look at it." Christian lays down to begin his reps.

Maybe they're right. I could try doing something out of my comfort zone. But I have a feeling that Henley won't really appreciate that type of thing. She's a no-nonsense woman, I can tell that just from spending a short amount of time with her.

No, I need to meet her on the territory we first bantered at. A keg, a party, somewhere she feels she has the upper hand. Janssen does have a point though, I'm not sure why I'm so hung up on this girl. I could just get under someone else to get over her. It might be worth it to do that.

Because Henley Rowan is going to be a hard nut to crack ... though she was smooth as velvet in my bed.

Even though I tell myself that I'll stop thinking about her, obsessing over why she hasn't returned any of my messages, I know I won't.

I'm going to get her to see me again.

R hiannon passes me a beer, and I grimace.

"This is all we have?"

"Sorry, couldn't score us any vodka tonight. Shitty beer it is." Rhiannon gulps some down.

Unfortunately, as freshman, we were left relying on whatever upperclassmen agreed to get us alcohol for the weekend. Sometimes, we scored big and got a whole handle of vodka that we could ration for a week or two. Other times, we were delivered a lowly twelve-pack of fifty-cents-a-can beer. And instead of the person either of us had originally texted to get it for us bringing it to our dorm room, it was like friend of a girlfriend's lab partner who dropped it off.

I can't wait until we turn twenty-one, though it's a ways off. And not like I'm a huge drinker, but it's college and I do it socially. Just like every other red-blooded American co-ed.

So, I pop open a can, take a drink, and wince as the bubbles hit my nose.

"Hey!" I exclaim, as Alden comes across the party toward me.

I'd mentioned we'd be coming to this party tonight. It's not one of the biggest ones I heard about happening on campus at this time, but I don't need to be showing up at any of the sporting houses. Lincoln is still sweating it out, as evidenced by the vague text he sent asking if I liked chocolates or flowers. Of course, I didn't answer, but it made me chuckle that he's debating resorting to cliché romantics.

I think after tonight I'll reel him back in, because we've both waited long enough to get into each other's pants. And I've strung him along just enough that he won't let me go so easily the next time I decide to grace him with my interest.

I know, I sound like a total frigid bitch. I've been going back and forth with myself, wondering if I can really do this. And then I'm reminded of all the girls I know he did the same thing to back home. Before Catherine, there were at least a few other girls I could remember that he ghosted or stood up after getting their panties wet. He deserves it.

Hugging Alden as he joins our twosome, I glance around the party. It's a different crowd, one with not so many hulking athletes, but more so, normal looking college kids. These are the ones who came for educational purposes, not to distract everyone on campus by their ridiculous looks and bodies.

"So glad you could make it. Want a beer?" I ask my photography friend.

"Sure." He shrugs; the arms of his tight black long sleeve forming nicely around his frame.

"Rhi, this is Alden," I introduce them, and see my roommate's eyes spark with interest.

In a second, it's gone though, replaced by a faux slyness that I know is an act. She's interested in him, but she's going to play hard to get. Atta, girl.

"And this must be Rhiannon." Alden sticks his hand out so that my roommate can shake it.

Rhiannon has a hard look on her face, with a tease of a

smile, when she daintily accepts his greeting. "Oh? You've been asking about me?"

I motion to Alden as if I've never told Rhiannon about him, even though I've gushed over how cute he is and how I think he's her type. I see my girl's game, she's playing hard to get, with just one toe in the water.

"Alden is in some of my photography courses. He saw the shoot I did with you and couldn't help but notice how pretty you are." I smile, threatening her with a "be nice" undertone.

"Beautiful. I believe I said beautiful." He sends her a dazzling smile.

Rhiannon's cool, aloof demeanor never waivers, and I seriously admire how hard she is. I'd be melting under Alden's megawatt charm if he was directing it at me. I guess I know a bit about that, though, warding off gorgeous guys that seem interested.

The music at the party turns up a notch, going from a poppy ballad to some hip-hop song Rhi has been blasting nonstop in our dorm room.

"Oh my God, I love this song!" She claps her hands and starts shaking her hips to the beat.

"Tory Lanez? Me too. Wanna dance?" Alden holds out his hand.

More people gather on the makeshift dance floor in the middle of the living room, and I watch as Rhiannon weighs her options. Finally, she takes his hand.

"Only if you can keep up." She smirks at him and drags him to the dance floor.

They disappear in a throng of people, leaving me on the sidelines grinning in accomplishment. I have a feeling I just played a great round of matchmaker. I sip my beer alone for a few minutes, content to just be and relax on a Saturday night.

A prickle of recognition tingles down my spine, and I turn.

Of course, he's here. There was no doubt he'd try to seek me out tonight, since I've not tried to contact him once.

Lincoln holds my eye contact as he swaggers across the room, the entire party splitting a walkway for him like he's freaking Moses in the Red Sea. Jesus Christ, does he look virile. Like sex on a stick. Dark jeans press against his thighs as he walks, and his dark locks are loose around his shoulders. He's like a brunette Chris Hemsworth, and my mouth goes dry just watching him walk. It's a sin, watching this man exist. Eve would certainly be in trouble if this guy was in her garden.

"You're a mighty hard girl to get ahold of." He dips his eyes, meeting mine on their level, when he reaches me.

Ah, so I'll get no small talk tonight.

I shrug. "I had to see if you were serious."

Lincoln's eyes startle with surprise. "The fact that I asked you to stay in bed wasn't evidence enough?"

My eyes roll so far back, I think they might stick. "How many girls have been in that bed before me? And how many have stayed the night for round two?"

If Lincoln is trying to maintain that I'm special because he allowed me to stay in his bed after we fucked, it'll be the first of many lies he tells me.

I'll make it about this. About his proving to me he's serious when he says he's interested in pursuing me. I won't point out my faults, or spill any secrets about how this was all a ploy to have him come crawling back, kissing the ring.

Lincoln sighs. "Listen, if you're not interested, just let me know. Don't do this whole games thing. I'm not into them. You don't want to hang out? Cool. Just don't ghost me. Be a little more mature than that."

His words hit me square between the eyes. Wow, I'm *stunned*. We've been doing nothing but playing games with our words and actions since the first day we met. And now he's hitting me with straight knowledge and chiding me about values. Talk about fucking a girl up; no college-aged male confronts women with logic and fairness.

"I'm interested," I say, not giving him anymore.

Mostly because he's stunned me into silence.

"Good. Because I'm interested, too." He sidles up to me. "Next time I text you, you'll text back?"

I take a long, slow sip of my beer, then turn to regard him. "Consider it done."

"And if I told you I'm taking you back to my room, what then?"

God, he's cocky. Showing up at this party intentionally to find me. Not mincing words about anything, throwing daggers at my heart. And now he's just completely bypassing the night and assuming I'll fall into bed with him again.

Which I will.

"I'd say let's go. I'm over this party."

Lincoln's smile is pure devilish, as if Hades himself whispered in the boy's ear all the naughty things he'd get to do to me tonight. My heart gallops with glee, while my vagina flutters with anticipation.

Phase two of my plan was in motion, but it didn't mean I wasn't going to get some really earth-shattering sex from it.

A week and a half passes in a blur of practices, games, class, and ...

Henley.

Every spare minute I have is dedicated to her. We passed that weird, initial stage of hooking up but not being attached, as evidenced by her refusal to return my messages. She claims she was undecided about whether I was a trustworthy guy, what with my jock background and all. And I'd overcome my wishy-washiness over linking myself to one girl.

And in the span of a week or so's time, we went from the casual hanging out and guessing what we were to full-on commitment without the title of it. When I wasn't practicing or in class, I was spending time with Henley. Whenever we were alone, we were shedding each other's clothes. If I could get a spare ten minutes, I was inside her.

Henley is one of the most intriguing girls I've ever met. Self-sufficient is her middle name, and while there can be a hardness about her, she's soft in the next instant. Her eye for beauty in the world, behind the lens of her camera, is magnificent. I often flip through her portfolio when she'll show it to me, marveling at the unique views in there. She's also fucking sexy. I've been with my fair share of girls, and sex is usually just a release for me. A fun way to feel pleasure. But with her ... it's more. I can't get enough of her. No matter how deep or hard or gentle or which position, I always yearn to taste her again. I always want to feel her explode around me again.

We were so hot and heavy that I could barely think about anything else.

Which is unfortunate, because I really need to get my head in this fucking game.

The crowd roars around us, thirty thousand people strong as the Saturday night lights beam down onto the turf. There is a grass stain on my pants, and a burn on my elbow from getting sacked that I'm pretty sure is bleeding.

Coach Daniels decided to play me the entire second half, which is a huge upgrade from our first two games where I only saw the last two drives of the game. It means I'm inching my way closer to that starting job. And if I can dig us out of the hole that Wayne got us into, I may able to solidify my spot.

"We're going with the Alaska, wide right, play. Make sure you know your coverage, skirt it, and get downfield, we need a big one here, guys. Let's fucking get it." I pump up my guys in a circle, as it's my job to execute and get this done.

We line up, the opposing team snarling in our faces. These guys made me look like an absolute rag doll two plays ago, and I'm not going to be made to look like an idiot any further.

I call for the snap, and everything blurs in motion. Helmets clank, players grunt, the fans boo and cheer accordingly. I block it all out, layering in on my receivers downfield. When one opens up, his coverage slipping their man, I rocket the ball toward him. Intuition sets in, and I know before he even catches it that it is going where I intend for it to land.

No more than five seconds later, the ball drops into his

hands, and he's off, down the field to the fifteen yard line, where a defender tackles him.

I hurry up the offense, waving them downfield and shouting the play call at the same time. We snap, but the defense read us too well. They scramble our play, and I'm about to get bowled over when I decide to make a run for it. I just need to get to the five yard line without getting my head ripped off, and I'm nearly there when one of their linemen comes at me, looking like I'm about to be his next meal.

Sprinting for the sidelines before he can tackle me and do damage, I don't realize I'm running right into the cheering section for Warchester.

I nearly run into one poor girl. The momentum from me running the ball to the sidelines has the cheerleaders scattering, and I try to jump over her like some kind of ninja, but she topples over from surprise.

"Shit! I'm sorry!" I throw the ball behind me for someone to catch now that the play is dead and crouch down to the cheerleader. "Are you okay?"

She shakes her head a little, bouncy brown curls moving in the big bow atop her skull. "I'm okay. You surprised me!"

The way she's able to flutter her lashes tells me that she's perfectly fine. I help her up and the crowd cheers as she presses into me. My spine goes rigid, but I don't back away, not wanting to cause a scene. I'm a figure for all of these people, their puppet who wins and walks around campus like an idol.

"Folks, let's give a round of applause for our quarterback, the Clark Kent of Warchester, Lincoln Kolb!" The announcer comes over the system, and the crowd erupts again.

I hold up a hand, waving.

"And now seems like the perfect time to start our Kiss Cam!" he says.

When I look up at the monitor, I see none other than my

own face up there. Next to the cheerleaders. I'm about to shake my head and laugh, to get back to the game. But then everyone is chanting my name, and I've never had this feeling before. Of so many people rooting just for me.

So I lean forward and plant a kiss on her cheek. She leans in, and I see us up on the camera, that perfect high school picture that so many teenage girls dream about. The football player and the cheerleader.

"Go get 'em champ!" she says, waving a pompom at me. "And afterward, hit me up."

I march back onto the field, adrenaline fucking coursing through my veins.

Half an hour later, I'm running off the field after winning my first game for Warchester. And there is only one place I'm going.

I'm keyed up from the game, the victory pulsing through my blood. It surges down to my balls, which are heavy with impending release. I'm always horny after a win, it's just the nature of the godlike feeling that seems to overtake athletes when they win a game.

In a few short minutes after arriving back to main campus, I'm in front of Henley's door, knocking insistently.

It opens slowly, to reveal a yoga-pant clad Henley with her hair tied up on her head, and a strappy tank top falling off her shoulders. Without a word, I push inside, my hands peeling the top down without hesitation. My tongue invades her mouth, but in another flash of a second, she's shoving my backward.

"You really are going to come in here and do that?" Henley practically spits, and I missed the rage in her coffee-colored eyes.

"What the ... ?" I'm so stunned by her reaction that I'm not processing fast enough.

"The Kiss Cam, really? You're pathetic. And then you have

the gall to come over here and shove your tongue down my throat? Get out."

Guilt gnaws at my stomach. "Jimmy, I'm sorry—"

"Don't call me that. Not when you just had to be the big man on campus. Did it feel good, getting your dick stroked by all of those people?" Henley is in a rage, and she misses me by a mile as she throws a small notebook across the room.

She's jealous. That shouldn't make me want to crack a smile, especially because she might decapitate me, but it does. She likes me enough that she's pissed about some other girl getting my affection.

"You're a cocky bastard, Lincoln. All you want is your ego inflated every second of the day—"

"Shut up," I demand.

Of course, she doesn't. "What the fuck, Lincoln? Don't ever say that to me. I'll kick you in the goddamn nu—"

I cut her off before she can follow through on that threat. "Shut up."

And then I crash my mouth right down onto hers. The kiss is angry and passionate, flames about to burst from our lips and light the whole room on fire. Her hands dive into my hair, pulling my face closer to hers, as I slide her tank top down all the way to her hips and roll her nipples between my hands.

"I came straight over here when we won." I breathe in between furious kisses. "The only one I want is you. That was a stunt, and I shouldn't have done it. I'm sorry."

My fingers push past her waistband, into her underwear, and down until I find her slick with desire. I push two fingers inside her and she all but screams.

"You. You're the one I want to fucking destroy me after I win. And you do. Every time."

Everything moves in fast forward after that. Clothes shed, moans unfurl from our mouths, we're tearing at each other like savage animals. Every inhibition is thrown out the window, and this is what make-up sex feels like. Anger dissipating into tormented need.

I track Henley like an animal, grabbing a condom from the place she keeps them beside her bed, and sliding it on. I don't even pause as she lies back, her hair surrounding her like a halo on the pillow, and I'm inside her before either of us can take our next breath.

Our eyes never leave the others as I fuck her, at first slow and deep and then gradually picking up the pace. Then it becomes a sprint, a marathon that leaves us both crying out in agonizing pleasure.

"Can't. You. See. I. Only. Want. You?" I grit out with every punishing thrust inside her.

She cries out, half-blind with all the pleasure I'm giving her. She grips at my back, her nails nearly drawing blood. The pain is so good; I push down farther onto her.

Like a rocket, Henley goes off, throwing her head back as she moans through the orgasm. I take the invite to latch my lips to her neck, and with her pussy still vibrating around me, I pour myself into the condom. It's the hardest I've ever come, the most intense sex I've ever had.

That? *That* was much more than sex.

It's the first moment I realize that I might not just be into this girl, but actively falling head over heels.

20

HENLEY

F all break comes before we know it.

Seven weeks into the semester, the school gives us a four-day weekend to ...

Well, I'm not really sure. Maybe go home and see our families? Study? Most people don't do either. Instead, they visit their friends who go to other colleges and get just as shit-faced as they do on a regular weekend at Warchester.

But we've decided to forego that and cross off one of my bucket list items instead. I finally confessed to Rhi what I've been doing, aside from the last item on the list concerning Lincoln. She was super supportive about it and even wanted to help.

Which is how two girls who barely like to squish a spider on their dorm wall ended up at a camping site in the middle of fucking nowhere.

"I'm going to kill you, Henley," Rhiannon mutters, lugging the portable stove we bought at the camping supply store out of her trunk.

"Not any more than I'm going to kill myself." I grin back

sarcastically in frustration, trying to read and understand the tent manual for the fiftieth time.

Why, Cat? Why did you have this on your list?

Rhiannon, Alden, and I were the first to arrive at our campsite. Even though she tells me he's her "friend" every time we talk about him, she and Alden have been having quite the courtship. And by that, I mean, as close to a relationship in college as one can come. Alden walks her to class every morning, they eat meals together, and four times now she's asked me to sleep at Lincoln's room when he is coming over. They're together, with everything but the title, as much as she wants to play nonchalant about it.

"You girls are wussies. This will be fun." Alden tries to push two of the metal poles of the tent together, but they bow and nearly smack him in the face.

"We're going to get eaten by bears, I just know it," Rhi whines, sitting down on the camping chairs I'd already set up around our designated fire.

I found this campsite, which is about an hour away from Warchester, online and paid for the spot with my credit card. I was ready to get this bucket list item over with, and as soon as I'd survived the night sleeping on dirt, I was going to book myself an extra-long spa manicure and pedicure.

A navy blue SUV pulls up alongside Alden's black truck, and Jamie hops out of the passenger seat. She brought with her a large Tupperware that I hope is filled with brownies, because it'd be the only way I was going to get through this.

"Hey!" she exclaims, giving me a hug. "Thanks for the invite. I love camping."

"That makes one of us." Rhiannon comes over and gives her a hug.

Jamie comes over to study almost once a week, so she and Rhi have already been acquainted.

"I hope it's okay I brought my ... guy." Jamie blushes.

She told me she's been hooking up with someone for about a month now, and I said of course she could bring him along. That makes me a fifth wheel, but I'm fine with it. This is going to be headache enough without feeling guilty about having Lincoln around to cross off a bucket list item. You know, when he *is* a bucket list item.

But I guess I should have asked who she was hooking up with, because when he gets out of the car, I about pee myself.

Shit, this is going to be so totally awkward.

"Wait, you're hooking up with him?" My eyes nearly bug out of my head as I see Lincoln's brawny friend carrying Jamie's tent.

She seems to stutter in her steps, blinks up at the guy, and then smiles nervously at me. "Um, yeah?"

"You didn't tell your friends about us?" Boulder-muscle guy looks seriously offended.

"This is Janssen. Janssen, this is Henley." Jamie makes introductions, but Janssen only looks like his jaw is about to unhinge.

"Wait, you're not that Henley—"

He's cut off when another body emerges from the big black truck, carrying a bunch of sleeping bags in hulking arms.

"So, who is ready to camp?"

Lincoln stands there in a flannel that makes his eyes pop way too beautifully, and a three-day-old scruff that I'd like to feel south of my waist. He looks like he could chop down a tree and then make his woman pancakes after ravishing her on the forest floor.

I swear, I almost drop the cardboard box of food I'm holding right onto my foot. I recover, only jostling it, while I stare open-mouthed at him.

"You're ... here? How, what ..." I sound like a blubbering fish, but I can't stop rambling.

There was a reason I didn't invite him on this trip. One, I

didn't want to embarrass myself. It's going to be hard enough for me to camp, seeing as I am so far from a nature girl that I think an evergreen scented candle is roughing it. But with him here? God, I would lose my entire cool girl persona, which is the whole facade for making me irresistible to him. If he sees how unnerved a night under the stars makes me, it'll tarnish some of the unreadable persona I've been building up to him.

And another reason? I needed some distance. We've been spending too much time together. He comes over almost every night, or I go to his room on the weekend. We grab meals together, or he sends me funny texts throughout the day. I know it's exactly what I wanted to happen, but I guess I didn't realize it would be such a ... relationship. Or that I'd look forward to seeing Lincoln every day after class.

He was beginning to grow on me, so much so that I forgot at times that I was doing this to ruin him. In those tender moments, when we were together in bed or laughing over lunch, it completely slipped my mind that I was ensnaring him in my web.

"Janssen told me he was going camping with his girl and her photography friend. Couldn't remember the name but said it started with an *H*. I thought I'd tag along, see if the friend was cute." Lincoln waggles his eyebrows at me sarcastically.

So, he knew I'd be here, and I didn't invite him to come. This was either going to be really awkward, or he'd brush it off after we had a talk.

After staring at the two of us for longer than needed, the other couples break off, pretending to busy themselves. I give Lincoln a weird smile, it even feels strange on my face, and go back to trying to set up my tent.

"Why didn't you ask me to come, Jimmy?" He crouches down where I'm hammering a spike into the ground.

"You have football." I don't meet his eyes.

"You knew I had a break in my football schedule." Lincoln's voice tells me just how silly my excuse sounds.

I chance a glance up at him and sigh. "I don't know? I-I'm not good at camping. Maybe I didn't want you to see it."

Lincoln lays a hand over mine so I stop working, so he can get to the root of the issue. Dammit, I hate how level-headed he is. I wasn't prepared for Lincoln Kolb to be so ... no nonsense. From his reputation, from what Catherine told me about him, I was expecting to get involved with someone who played games even when he was in a fully-committed relationship. Days without talking, skirting around issues, not giving straight answers, not caring if I disappeared—these were the things I thought Lincoln would pull.

It unnerves me that he's so genuine. That he wants to get down to the core of the problem so we can move forward. It makes me like him more, which I simultaneously loathe. It pisses me off that I can't hate him more.

"Well, we can address why you're camping when you hate it later. But that's not the reason. I think you're scared. Of this." He motions back and forth between the two of us.

God, I hate that he thinks he can read me so well. And I freaking hate that that is actually the reason, and he knows it.

"I thought you'd be going home, or spending time with other people. You've been with me a lot lately." Why am I pushing him away?

I should be relishing in his attention, wanting him to be all over me and all about me. That's part of the plan. Get him hooked. We're past the stage where I need him to chase me, because from all angles it appears that Lincoln is only about me. He said as much after the whole Kiss Cam incident, where he all but freaking branded me with his cock. God, that sex had been *amazing*. He was so intense about it, so pissed off that I questioned him.

I have him right where I want him. And yet, I'm getting cold feet. Maybe I don't want to follow through on breaking his heart. Maybe I'm just scared I'll break my own. Either way, I'm doing the opposite of what I should right now, and it only adds to my complicated feelings about the whole thing.

"And that's a bad thing?" Lincoln smirks like he sees right through me. "Come on, Henley, just admit you're freaked out that we spend almost every day together. That you didn't invite me on this trip because it turned into a couple's thing, and then you'd have to call us a couple. Am I right? Because I know I am."

Notice he didn't say he thinks he's right. He said he knows. Jeez, he's so confident. I both love and loathe it.

I sweep a piece of hair behind my ear and give him a small smile. "It's annoying how right you are. Isn't it the woman's job to always be right?"

"We can both be right if you just stop disagreeing with me." Lincoln grins.

"Aren't you freaked out by how much time we've been spending together?" I ask, curious.

Lincoln shakes his head. "No. I wasn't looking for anything, but I'm not mad we fell into this."

Not the most romantic sentiment, but at least he's here when he could have spent his break fucking random girls. I know he could have. So does he. And I need him here to complete my last bucket list item, though my heart is denying that's happening.

"You're not mad we fell into this?" I raise an eyebrow.

Lincoln grabs my waist, gently tickling. "Don't give me shit about my wording when you didn't even invite me on the camping trip. What I'm trying to say is, I'm all in. How about you?"

Fuck. It annoyed me how to the point he was.

"I'm all in." I nod, both elated and disconcerted at the flutter that passes through the organ in my chest.

Lincoln leans forward, capturing my chin with his hand and laying his lips over mine. The kiss is gentle, a whisper, a promise.

It leaves me breathless, and I can barely open my lids when he pulls back.

"Now, let me build this tent, because if you do it, we'll definitely be getting eaten by a wild animal out in the open tonight."

"Won't that happen anyway?" I smirk.

"Right now, there is about a fifty percent chance. But with a proper tent built by your man, it'll lower to about thirty."

I roll my eyes. "I need a snack anyway. I deserve it after all the hard work. Besides, you have more fat on you than I do. They'll eat you first."

As I walk away, I hear Lincoln laughing wholeheartedly.

"Never have I ever swam naked in a lake."

Janssen's eyebrows wiggle as he looks at everyone around the circle. I shrug, keeping my beer balanced on my knee as Lincoln adjusts his arm that's been cradling me into his side. He takes a swig, not making eye contact with me.

"You have?" I laugh, staring at him.

"Bastard did that because he knows I have." Lincoln sends a middle finger to his best friend. "It was one year at football camp, we did it as a dare on the last night."

"So it was just a bunch of naked football players in a lake? That I'd like to see." Rhiannon cackles.

But to everyone's surprise, Jamie drinks, too.

"Babe, what?" Janssen cries out, but his eyes spark with lust.

Lincoln's best friend from home is not a person Catherine ever told me about. Not because we didn't gossip about our respective high schools, but because in her last year on earth, we just didn't bother with it. She found out she was sick in October, and Lincoln dumped her shortly thereafter. So while I heard her gush about the quarterback all summer, she didn't really bother telling me about his friends. And then, when he broke her heart, we only talked about how much of an ass he was, and how much we wanted revenge.

Jamie shrugs. "It was a dare, just like Lincoln said."

"Show me. Show me right now." Janssen stands up, and starts to unbuckle his pants.

She pulls at him, bringing him back down onto the bench they're sharing. "Sit down, hornball. It's about twenty degrees in that late. You go in there and your balls will definitely shrivel to nothing."

He sits down, his eyes wide. "You're so right. What would I do without you, babe?"

"Okay, Alden's turn." Rhiannon turns to her guy.

Alden smiles. He's quieter than Janssen or Lincoln, the latter of whom apologized for how curt he was the first time he met him. But he's still engaged, mostly with trying to get Rhiannon to lean into him more. He's managed to get his arm around her, though my roommate is maintaining her aloof independence.

"All right." He looks to be thinking. "Never have I ever ... kissed two people in one night."

A chuckle goes through the group, and most everyone drinks, Lincoln and I included.

"My turn!" Rhi claps her hands, then picks her drink up off the ground. "Never have I ever been in love."

An awareness passes over, and leave it to her to do that. What a little shit, though I love her. No one aside from Jamie and Alden drink, and I peek up at Lincoln.

His eyes are already looking down at me when I sneak a glance, and we both smile a shy grin. So, he's never been in love. Neither have I, but I'm wondering if he might be on his way there when it comes to me. I hope so. The sooner I can stop this charade, the better.

We're dangerously close to both being decimated. Damn you, Catherine.

"And with that, I'm exhausted," Jamie says, rising. "Time to call it a night?"

"The sooner we can get out of this fucking campsite, the better," Rhi agrees, pulling Alden up by the hand and leading them to their tent.

Lincoln and I stay back, cleaning up as the moonlight filters through the trees around us. Every so often, I catch him looking at me, our gazes locking across the clearing.

When I started this, pursuing him and putting this plan in action, I never expected to crash and burn quite as hard as I am for Lincoln Kolb. I knew it would be messy, what with what Catherine told me about his charm. But this is ... something more. There is a prickle of awareness that he's never felt this way about anyone, and I haven't either. Not the way we feel about each other.

After all the trash is picked up and the fire is smoldering into embers, he wraps his arms around me and walks us toward our tent. There isn't even a question of sleeping separately, we both know it would be a pointless discussion.

We undress together, pulling on warmer clothes, and then Lincoln arranges our sleeping bags so that they're both unzipped, one on the floor and the other thrown over us like a comforter.

"It's too cold," I whine, burrowing my nose into the crook of Lincoln's neck as we settle in.

Maybe it wasn't such a bad idea to have him here. He's like a furnace next to me, and I won't have to fend off wild cats all by myself if they come knocking on the tent door.

The sounds of the night surround us, the hoot of owls and what I hope are not the growls of bears.

"Why the hell did you agree to camp if you hate it?" Lincoln chuckles, snuggling in closer to me.

I'm too distracted by his warm, naked muscles that my tongue slips. "I made a promise to a friend."

He raises an eyebrow. "To go camping? And why is said friend not here with us?"

I freeze, trying to seem nonchalant, all the while my internal panic system is blaring an alarm. "Uh, well ... it's a long story."

He nods, chewing on his lip. "How come every time I try to learn some small piece of information about you, you clam up?"

Hmm, I hadn't realized he'd realized that. I guess I'm not doing as great of a job throwing him off my scent as I thought I was.

"I don't know, it just seems dumb to talk about a promise I made. Thought we were moving forward, not back?" I challenge him.

"But to move forward, I want to know more about you. Where did you grow up, what's your favorite Christmas present you ever got? Why are you sleeping in a bag on the ground if you hate it?" Lincoln palms my ass, not above copping a feel even during a serious conversation.

It feels so good, the sensual massage, that my tongue loosens in the process.

I sigh. "I grew up not far from here, in a town called Little Port."

Lincoln jerks up, resting on an elbow. "Wait what? No way! I grew up in Winona Falls."

"Really?" I try to feign surprise.

It's a risk, telling him where I grew up. Especially with my proximity to Catherine. But nothing registers in his face. There is no flicker of ever having seen me in town or randomly out at the mall the two municipalities shared.

"How weird is that. All this time, and you were just a town over." Lincoln lies back down, stumped, and puts our foreheads together. "So, what else?"

I kiss the tip of his nose. "My favorite Christmas present was this trip my parent's got me to New York City when I was fourteen. They took me to the Met, and a bunch of photography exhibits around the city. It was perfect."

Just thinking about that trip makes me itch to go back to the Big Apple. The sights, the sounds; the city was a living, breathing art project.

"And I'm sleeping on the ground in a bag because I made a promise to a friend that I won't see for a while." I shrug it off like this will explain it and then launch into a question. "How about you, what was your favorite Christmas present ever?"

Lincoln snorts. "Easy. The football they put in my hands at age five."

I roll my eyes, even though he can't see them in the dark. "Of course."

We fall asleep in the wee hours of the morning, questions still on our tongues and so much of our personalities talked out.

I'm eating lunch with Henley when my phone rings, Mom's face lighting up the screen.

"Do you mind?" I ask, trying to be polite.

Henley shakes her head, forking a piece of strawberry in her goat cheese salad. "Go ahead."

The sounds of the campus cafe, the one you have to use bonus points or real money to eat in, carry on around us. It's a Tuesday, which means our schedules line up to eat together, and she has a weakness for that salad. I get it for her every time, using the unlimited meal points I get as a student athlete.

"Mom, hey," I say, picking up.

"She was drunk." Her voice almost cracks, but I can tell she's trying to keep it together.

"What?" My tone is too harsh, but I can't help it.

"The kids showed up for their second scheduled visitation, and she was drunk. Brant said Cheryl smelled funny, and that she couldn't talk right. Tyla said she was falling asleep. The supervisor cut the visit short, but not before the kids were thoroughly freaked out. I could spit nails, Lincoln ..."

Mom is clearly in distress, as she typically liked to keep me out of the loop and focused on football and school. If she was calling me to vent, she was at the end of her rope. The entire custody matter was stressing us all out, and I knew she was just having a real tough time. Mom was with Tyla and Brant more than anyone, so she wanted to see them in a loving, caring environment.

"*Motherfucker*," I curse, and then look up to see Henley staring at me. I wince, mouthing an apology. "That should make a better case against her though, right?"

Mom sighs. "That's what we're hoping. It's horrible it had to happen this way, but it's better for the kids in the long run. I can't believe she showed up like that. Those kids worship the ground she walks on, and for her to do that ... I just don't know how you abandon your children like that."

"Addiction is a disease, but I hate that. I hate that she gets to use it as an excuse," I grunt out, trying to keep my voice down.

Though I know Henley is fully eavesdropping on the conversation.

"I love you, sweetheart, I hope you're having a good day," Mom says, trying to lighten her tone.

"Thanks, Mom. I'm actually having lunch with um, Henley," I say, sheepishly looking across the table.

I'm not sure if she's told her folks about me yet, but I've told my parents about Henley. She's the first girl I've been serious about, and my family doesn't keep secrets from each other.

"Oh, good!" Mom practically squeals. "Tell her I say hi, and that we'd love to take her out after this weekend's game if she'd like to come to dinner with us."

"Okay, I'll tell her." I nod, and Henley's face is full of curious amusement. "Love you, Mom."

"Love you, buddy. I'll let you know if I hear anything else from the courts. Bye."

I hang up and immediately realize I'm going to have to explain some things about that call.

"Told your mom about me, huh?" She smirks into her salad.

"Yeah, I told her how hot you are in bed. How when I do that thing with my tongue—"

"Oh my God, stop!" Her face is as red as a lobster, and the outburst has other tables looking at us.

Mission accomplished.

I pick up her hand where it lays on the table and lace my fingers through hers. "Yes, I told my mom about you. We don't keep secrets. She wants you to come to dinner with us after the game this week."

Henley looks squirmy. "Hmm, okay."

That isn't an answer, but I'll push her later. Everything with this girl is greasing wheels, but I kind of like that about her. I wouldn't want someone who so easily complied with whatever I wanted.

"So, do you want to know what I was talking about?" I ask, treading into unfamiliar waters.

Henley looks straight into my eyes. "Only if you want to tell me."

Telling her this ... it lets her into the most vulnerable part of my world. Of me. This is something I haven't even shared with my closest friends, so telling the girl I'm involved with? That gives our relationship a whole other layer.

Our relationship? Is this a relationship? I guess I'm now thinking of it in terms of yes, it is. We spend every night together, plan our weekends around each other, she comes to my games; I buy her coffee before I walk her to class. It's a damn relationship.

But is Henley ready for this? The next layer, to go deeper? I know she's been struggling with her feelings for me, it's plain as day. Where I'm a bit shocked that I fell this hard for a girl this early, I'm going with the flow. I've always been the kind of guy to adapt, to see where the play takes me, but clearly, my girl is not. She is resisting with every step of the way. From the initial hookup and then ghosting me, to not letting me keep a pair of gym shorts in her dorm room, to getting pissed about the Kiss Cam, to not inviting me on the camping trip.

She's scared as hell, and I'm trying to soothe her fears with every spook she gets. Because I care about her, a ton. Because we're good together, and she knows it too. So I'm not going to let her chicken out because she thinks I'm a jock or because this is first semester of freshman year, and these relationships are notorious for blowing up in people's faces. Nine times out of ten, first semester flings are just that; an exciting, "I just got out of my parent's house" blazing display of adultness that isn't actually adult at all.

That's not what we are though. I feel it down to my bones. We're the real deal.

"I have two cousins on my Mom's side, they're my aunt Cheryl's kids. Tyla and Brant, she's four and he's eight. And they're amazing, just the coolest little kids you've ever met. Anyways, my parents are trying to adopt them, have been trying for almost two years."

I had been looking down at my hands, trying to get the story out without letting my anger or emotion cloud it. But when I look up at Henley, she's focused right on me, a sadness in her coffee-colored eyes. I hold on to her hand tighter.

"My aunt is an addict, has been running around in the wrong circles with the wrong guys with the wrong substances for years. She's never given those kids a damn ounce of the attention, love, and support they deserve, but she's been fighting to keep custody of them. God knows why; she's completely unfit. She's never cared about anyone but herself." I can feel my blood pressure start to rise at a rapid rate.

"People always want what they can't have," Henley says quietly.

I nod. "And she's been fighting hard. Even though Mom and Dad can give her children a life that they'd never get with her. Anyway, she had a supervised visit with them today. Showed up drunk. And even though that's good for our case—"

"It still causes a ton of unneeded stress and upset for your little cousins," Henley finishes my sentence.

I know in that instant that it was a good idea to tell her. She understands the gravity of the situation without even having to know more details. This girl is simply ... perfect. For me.

"Exactly. So, hopefully, this will turn things in my parents' favor and finally bring this process to an end. The kids are just ... they're amazing. They don't deserve this."

A beat passes, and then Henley gets up from her chair. She walks around our table, bends down, and plants a kiss on my lips.

"You're a good man, Stallion."

I'm not sure anyone has ever called me that. But coming from Henley's mouth, I believe it more than anything I've ever believed about myself.

A couple hours later, I'm waiting for Henley to come out of the communications building.

She's been in the photo lab for hours, having reserved the darkroom for developing, and I don't like it when she walks home alone so late in the evening. She tells me I'm crazy, but I've heard crazier stories about girls who walk home alone on campus at eleven thirty at night. So, if she's working until midnight, I usually come down here and escort her home.

Secretly, I know she thinks it's chivalrous, which is half the reason I do it. Any excuse to make that girl think more highly of me, I'll take it.

As I'm scrolling through my Twitter feed, looking at commentary of this week's news in both professional and college football, my phone rings. Henley's name appears on the screen, and I pick it up.

"Hey, you coming up?"

"Actually, can you come down? I need some help carrying things." She sounds preoccupied.

"Sure, be right there."

I take the stairs down to the bottom level of the building and guess my way around. I'm never really here aside from when I walk Henley to and from class, since my major has no lectures on this area of campus. So I'm basically banking on the fact that I don't get lost, and when I see an arrow pointing in the direction of the photo lab, I follow it.

Wandering into a large, lofted room with lots of lit up tables, I don't see Henley.

"Jimmy?" I call out, feeling eerie.

I didn't see anyone on my way here, though I don't doubt there are other students working in these classrooms late into the night. That's just college for you. But I won't pretend to be a strapping man and say I'm not spooked that we're here in the dark, alone.

A door opens to a pitch black room, and Henley's blond curls catch my eyes. "In here, hurry, I have photos developing."

The door is practically shut by the time I reach it, moving quickly inside. My eyes are met with a red light, an obnoxious smell, and a lot of photos hung up on strings above my head.

"Jesus, it smells terrible in here." I clap a hand over my nose.

Henley chuckles. "I'm so used to it by now that it doesn't even bother me. If you want, there are masks over there."

She points to a pile of surgical masks, but I've always hated wearing those things. Plus, if she can stand it, so can I.

"What're you working on? You need help?" I move to her, not able to resist the need to touch her.

My hand goes to the small of her back, and I lean into her, smelling the lavender scent of her shampoo which drowns out the solution she's working in the tub over her photos.

Henley looks up at me, her eyes sheepish. "I didn't really need help moving anything. I just heard a noise and got spooked."

"And needed a strong, brave man to come down and protect

you?" I make a muscle with my free arm, all but kissing the bicep.

She rolls her eyes, ignoring me. "Plus, I wanted to show you this."

The tongs she's using to swoosh the photo paper around in the solution begin to reveal the image she wants me to see. Slowly but surely, as she takes it out of the chemicals and pins it up onto the string, I see the outline of my uniform.

It begins to come more clearly into focus. Me, in the middle of my teammates, directing them on the upcoming play. Even though my helmet is on, you can still see my eyes, and they're intense but engaged. You can tell, from this photograph, how much I love the game of football. Henley captured me in my rawest form, and somehow told the story of my life in one snapshot.

I turn her, holding her hips until they're flush against mine, and then bring my mouth down to hers. Henley's tongue is lazy as it meets mine, our lips nibbling and testing as we gyrate slowly against each other. There is no music, but here we are, dancing to a sexual rhythm only our ears can hear.

The kiss picks up, heating until it's at boiling level. I want to push aside the tubs on the table, take her right here, but have no idea what chemicals I'd be splashing onto the floor.

I break off, resting my forehead against hers. "As much as it would be sexy as hell to fuck you, right here in this room, I don't want us getting third-degree burns from anything on these tables."

Henley chuckles. "I've had fantasies about doing it in here, but I agree, we might not want to get busy with this stuff nearby."

"Plus, it stinks." I kiss her nose. "You done? Can we go hurry back to my dorm now?"

Because if I couldn't do it in here, I wanted to fuck the shit out of her in my bed.

"Take me home, Stallion."

She doesn't have to tell me twice.

L incoln starts his first game just days after telling me about Tyla and Brant and takes the Warchester team to victory.

Like it or not, I now know all I need to about football and more. I know the ways that players get penalties, what a first down means, and how many points a field goal is worth. I attend pretty much every home game and even traveled with Rhiannon to the last two away games that were over an hour in the car listening to Drake and Lil Wayne the whole way.

So when I sit down at the table, at Warchester's nicest Greek restaurant, I feel like I already kind of know Lincoln's family.

Scratch that, I feel like I know them because the Kolbs are one of the *it* families in Winona Falls, and Catherine along with everyone else talked about them constantly growing up. They attend the right church, his mom hosts the raffle nights at the high school each year, Lincoln and his brother practically ran the sports scene in their first eighteen years on earth.

I have to cross my fingers that no one in their family recognizes my last name, but I doubt they will. My little family is pretty low-key when it comes to social events around our town or the next one over.

"And then he came downstairs wearing his father's tux, it was so long I thought he'd fall headfirst down the stairs." Lincoln's mom, Justine, cracks up, her laugh infecting me.

"Stop it, that is too funny." I hold my chest, gasping as I laugh.

She was telling the story about the first time Lincoln had a crush on a celebrity, Mariah Carey, and he dressed up in his father's tuxedo thinking he could go track her down and profess his undying love.

"Hey, 'Always Be My Baby' was a great song." Lincoln shrugs, not embarrassed at all.

"Still is," I agree, popping a piece of falafel in my mouth.

"Ew, why did you eat that?" Brant, the little boy Lincoln had told me about, screws up his face.

"It's really good. If you try some, I'll play tic-tac-toe with you again," I challenge him.

He eyes me, skeptical. Then pops a piece in his mouth. Chews. Assesses. And smiles.

"It's good. And you're on!" He frantically draws another game board on his kid's menu.

We've been playing tic-tac-toe for the duration of the meal, as opposed to Tyla, who has just shown me every doll in her backpack for an hour. They're both so cute, I'm not sure how these people ever get through a day without turning into heart-eye emojis.

"Henley, Lincoln tells me you're a photographer?" His dad, Vincent, asks.

I nod. "Yes, hoping to learn all I can at Warchester and then start my own business when I graduate."

"He's sent me a couple of your photographs from Instagram, they're wonderful," Justine praises me.

I look to Lincoln, who is smiling at me in that shy way that makes my heart flip over and then sprint a marathon. He showed her my photographs.

"Thank you. I work hard on them." I never shy away from compliments when it comes to my work.

I know how good I am. Anyone who ever tries to brush off their talents or passion is just selling themselves short, and I won't do that.

"Maybe you can take our picture! Like a movie star!" Tyla gushes, scooting closer to my side.

"I'd love to." I smile at her.

"You might break her lens, you're too beautiful." Lincoln tickles his cousin.

Watching Lincoln with not only his family, but his two little cousins? Jesus, my heart can't take it. It's like the guy is composing a résumé for catch of the year. If I didn't already think the guy had no flaws, this would be the icing on the perfect cake.

He's kind with their childish minds, never mocking them or brushing them off but indulging in every one of their silly games and weird conversation topics. At the same time, he's respectful of his parents and keeps the whole meal flowing, engaging me in the talk their having while highlighting my interests to his family. Lincoln Kolb was blessed with the whole package, and I'd hate him for it if I wasn't falling in love with him.

Falling in love with him? *Fuck*. That wasn't supposed to happen.

"So, Linc, anymore buzz from the agents?" Vincent asks.

Lincoln shushes his father. "Dad, you know I'm not supposed to be talking to those guys."

His mom rolls her eyes. "We know that. The whole world knows that. Doesn't mean it doesn't happen. We just want to know what's going to happen with your career."

Lincoln sighs, relenting. "Yes, I've had some interest. But it's too early. I have two more years."

"And in two more years, you'll be the first pick of the draft, mark my words." His dad claps him on the back.

Surprise flutters through me. I mean, I know Lincoln is great at football. I don't even know much about the sport and I can see, by watching him play, that he's head and shoulders above the other guys on the field. Both on his team and the opposing teams. But I guess we have never talked about his future. I'm so focused on not slipping up, on seeming mysterious and hooking my claws into him that I've ...

Missed one of the biggest things about the guy who is sleeping in my bed every night.

"You're going to go pro?" I ask him.

His mom and dad look surprised, but Lincoln just laughs. "She knows nothing about football. It's one of the things I like most about her. And yes, I'm going to go pro. I'll probably declare my junior year, which means I won't finish college. It's not what I want to do anyway. I'll get drafted and play for a team. Hopefully, win a few rings. Super Bowl rings, that is."

I could just see it now. Lincoln Kolb, star athlete, all over the sports channels and the regular morning shows. He'd be their shining light, the charismatic hotshot with a zillion screaming female fans. There will be nowhere I can't escape his face.

Which, when I break his heart, will be pretty unfortunate for me. But he'll move onto a bigger, brighter life. He'll meet a hundred girls in a hundred different cities who will come at the crook of his finger.

And that sends a pang of sadness through me. Suddenly, I don't feel much like eating.

The rest of the meal goes great, but something inside me is off. I hadn't thought much about what happens after this. How

I'll have to see him, how I'll wonder what he's doing and with who.

I never thought about how we'll mend separately after I tear us apart.

"I win. Drink."

Lincoln looks at me, his eyes glazing over from the three beers he's already had, and winks.

God, this boy is much too handsome for his own good.

"I know I am." He grins.

"What?" I ask, the music messing with my ears.

"You just said I'm much too handsome for my own good. I said I know I am." He rounds the table where we're playing quarters and scoops me off my feet.

Shit, did I say that out loud? I must be drunker than I think I am.

We're at yet another party at the football house, but this is the first one I've been to where Lincoln and I are actually together. He's had his hands all over me for most of the night, and if he's not careful, I may just drag him up to the bathroom we first made out in.

As it is, I'm practically straddling his waist before he pins me to a wall.

"Jesus, how drunk did you two get while we were gone?" Rhiannon snorts, Alden at her back.

They have been tearing up the dance floor most of the night. I'm actually surprised at his moves, and how much he keeps up with her.

"Catch up," I dare her, cackling.

Lincoln puts me down. "I have to take a leak."

"Ew, I hate when guys say that." I scrunch up my nose.

His only answer is to grab my chin, pull it toward him and hit me with such a searing kiss that I stagger sideways the minute he releases me.

"Woah. Someone is getting lucky tonight. Should I put a scrunchie on the door?" Rhi jokes.

"Yeah, go to Alden's." I don't even look at her, all of my energy focused on Lincoln, who is walking backward down the hall in an attempt to seduce me.

Five minutes go by, in which I take another shot with Rhiannon and play a round of quarters with her and Alden. We're all laughing when I zero in on something happening in the living room.

Lincoln, leaning against a wall, while a brunette in six-inch heels presses her tits into him.

Jealousy surges through me, a fiery hot branding iron that someone has shoved down my throat and won't let up on. Here I am, having sex with him almost every night, and he's still out chasing tail. Is that the most cliché man stereotype ever, or what?

Looking closer, I see her hand on his chest. The way she leans in to try to nuzzle his ear. Lincoln steps back, distancing himself, but she keeps coming. Ah, I see what's happening here. She's trying to claim him, whether she's heard about me or not doesn't matter. And he's ... being a good guy. Trying to easily brush her off, not embarrass her. He's respecting what he has with me, when I could have very well caught him with his hand down her skirt.

But isn't this how it will always be? If I abandoned Catherine's list, if I allowed myself to be with Lincoln for real, wouldn't he always be hit on like this? Of course he will. It's just who he is, it's how bright his star shines. Do I want to be with someone I constantly have to worry about either cheating, or being the object of gossip and rumors?

Maybe it's the alcohol, and maybe I'm just tired of living my double life, but an idea sneaks in.

Break up with him tonight.

It takes me by surprised at first, and my heart protests it from the start. But once I sink into it more, like a spiky arm chair or that throne from that HBO show Catherine used to love, I realize just how great of an idea it is.

One, I'm drunk, so it won't hurt me as much. Two, it has to happen sooner or later. Three, I'm pretty sure it will gut Lincoln, so the item can be crossed off the bucket list.

It's better this way, ending it right here and right now. If we move any further, any deeper, the fallout will be catastrophic. I'll just put a stop to things, blame it on him talking to this girl. It's a convenient excuse, one I can fall back on later. Sure, Lincoln will probably be fucking pissed, may even try to fight me on it, but in the end, things will fizzle with the awkwardness and unsure nature of a first semester of freshman year relationship.

Lincoln is the type of guy who tells his mom about me. He buys my favorite coffee to pick me up from class with. When I need a drink of water after coming home from a party, he's the one who runs to the bathroom to get it. Lincoln is everything I'd ever dreamed a boyfriend (though he's not my boyfriend) could be, and it's getting harder and harder to separate that from the guy Catherine said he was.

If I don't get out soon, I'm going to be the one with a broken heart.

Marching right up to him, I set my game face on.

"What the hell are you doing?" I push him, and the scene has started.

The girl who had her paws on him scampers off, clearly not wanting to be in the middle of this, and Lincoln looks gobsmacked.

"Jimmy, it wasn't what it looked like. She came onto me, I was trying to get back to you—"

I cut him off. "That's what they all say! You were just waiting for me to turn my back so you could mack on some other chick. You're pathetic, Lincoln!"

I push him, adding to the drama. Maybe if I piss him off enough, he won't even want to fight for us. Maybe he'll just cut his losses and walk, make this easy on me.

Instead, Lincoln does just the opposite. He reaches for me. "Hey, don't do that. It isn't like that and you know it. I'm with you. I only have eyes for you."

"Yeah, until a stripper in heels comes along!" I motion to said stripper, and the poor girl cowers. "Stay away from me, Lincoln. We're done."

I emphasize my statement with a stomp and then turn on my heel. And for as drunk as I thought I was, I'm painfully sober now. The crack of my heart is audible to my own ears, and I feel like I might throw up. Not from the drinking, but from the bone deep sadness piercing my body.

The only thing I want to do now is crawl into my bed and bawl my eyes out.

I knew it would be hard to disentangle myself from Lincoln Kolb.

I had no idea it would devastate me on every level of my soul.

"Hey! *Hey*, would you stop? Henley!"

I'm chasing her down the sidewalk, other college students littering various lawns from the parties that have spilled out onto them. They glance at us, the guy yelling at the girl who is retreating, but they do nothing. It's probably a common scene out here on a Saturday night.

She's speed walking away from me, even in those heeled boots that look like her ankle is going to break every time she takes a step. How girls walk in those things is beyond me.

"Jimmy!" I shout her nickname, and my footsteps pick up until I reach her completely.

My hand shoots out, grasping her elbow, and she spins. "Don't touch me!"

My God, she's dramatic. And completely fucking beautiful when she's this angry. I basically want to mount her in the street.

"Will you just stop? You're being ridiculous." I roll my eyes, the alcohol I've already consumed loosening my tongue.

By the fire I just lit in Henley's eyes, I know it's the exact wrong thing to say at this moment. Never tell a pissed off drunk girl you're trying to win back that she's ridiculous.

"Fuck you, Lincoln. Don't tell me I'm being dramatic when you were the one all over some slut back there!" She points her finger violently toward the house.

I try to take a calming breath. "Stop it, I wasn't. That's not what happened at all."

"You seemed awfully friendly back there." Henley's voice is scary levels of high pitched.

"She is in one of my education classes. I was answering a question!" I throw my hands up.

Because I was. And because I was trying to get her grabby hands off me and return to my girl, to put my grabby hands all over *her*. It's not my fault some girl mauled me, and Henley knows it. But she's putting on this show right now, and I can't quite figure out why.

"With your dick? Because I'm pretty sure that's the answer she wanted!" Henley shouts again, and the people around us are staring and giggling.

I hug her to me, though she tries to struggle, and walk us down to a more secluded part of the sidewalk. All I want to do is close my mouth over hers, get her to shut up. Because once we're kissing, she'll forget all of this nonsense.

"I thought we were over this stage. This unsureness. I'm with you, Henley." I try to look her in the eyes, but she won't meet mine.

"Whatever, Lincoln, we're done. Whatever this is, I'm not doing it anymore! I don't want to be some side piece while jersey chasers flock around you at all moments! I'm a fucking catch!" She throws her arms out, as if she needs to be on top of some soapbox saying this.

"We're not done. Not even close to it," I growl, pissed off that she's even throwing the thought out into the universe.

"Yes, we are!" She stomps her foot like a child.

My shoulders rise a couple inches. "No, we're not."

"Yes." She juts her chin out.

"No." I'm inches from her lips.

And then it all clicks. She's not jealous, she's scared.

Of what this could really turn into. Of how serious we could get, since we were on the way there. Henley fought me tooth and nail from the beginning, I've fought for every yard of territory I've gained with her. And I wanted to, fight that is. She's worth it.

We're worth it.

I didn't think I'd need to get romantic with a girl like Henley, but apparently, that's exactly what she needs to close the deal. So, I clear my throat, put on my best romance hat, and let the flowery language flow.

"I didn't do this before because I didn't think it was needed. It's been pretty clear to me from the start that you're the girl I want to spend all my time with. And to be honest, I hate having those awkward 'what are we' conversations. No guy likes to have them. But I'll do it, because you mean that much to me."

Henley sucks in a breath, but doesn't interrupt me.

"From the minute I saw you, I knew what unfolded between you and me would be much more than anything I've ever felt for another girl. You're special, Henley, and that sounds cliché, but it's true. You're tough and independent, while hiding your softer side from anyone who doesn't deserve to know it. But when you show that side to me, *Christ*, it melts my fucking heart. You're sexy without trying, you have that natural kind of beauty that shines from every inch of your skin. I could lay in bed and look at you all day long, and still never be tired of it. When you work, you're a phenom. Watching you photograph your subjects is like watching art being created; you're so focused and intense, and you do a hell of a job. And the way you are with me, taking all of my shit and handing it right back on a silver platter? I've never had that before. You call my bluff, you make me laugh, you are the one I want to wrap my arms around at the end of the day.

When we're drunk at a party, the only girl I want to grab my junk is you. The only girl I want asking me to take their boots off in my dorm room because she's too drunk is you. Don't you get it, Henley? I want you to be my girlfriend. I didn't ask before because I thought you'd be spooked by the label, but now I see it for what it is. You're scared that without it, we don't have a definite thing going on. I'm here to tell you that what we have is a relationship, a concrete one. You're my girlfriend. I'm your boyfriend. And if you don't like it, tough. That's what is happening."

And I mean every word of it.

When I'm done, she's standing in front of me with tears glistening in her eyes. I pray to God they're ones of happiness, and not the kind that mean she's about to crush my heart under the heel of her sexy boot.

"I'm scared," she whispers, so much emotion in her voice.

Sliding a piece of hair behind her ear, I palm her cheek. "I know you are."

"What if I hurt you?" Henley's lip quivers.

"Then you do. And we work through it. I'm not saying there won't be days where I piss you off. Of course, there will be. But I want them all the same. I want you."

After what feels like an eternity of her staring into my eyes, unsure, she finally speaks.

"Okay."

I blink once, then twice. "What?"

"I said, *okay*. I'll be your girlfriend." She nods.

I don't give her a second to take it back. Instead, I haul her up, sitting her on my hips, and fuse my mouth to hers.

I may or may not walk us all the way back to the dorms and up to my room in that exact position.

I t's a rare night when Lincoln decides studying is more important than going out, but alas, tonight is such a night.

"This is so boring," he whines, flopping back on my pillow.

We're sitting on my bed, at opposite ends, with books stretched between us. Lincoln has been complaining every few minutes, throwing his books and trying to distract me. He's literally the worst study partner I've ever had, but he's so freaking gorgeous that I can't really be mad.

The only reason he decided to stay in tonight, and convinced me to do so too by bribing me with calzones and sex, is because he has a huge exam coming up in one of his education courses. Midterms are coming up, and almost everyone on campus is bugging out. Not me, though. I'm doing so well in my courses that I don't need to worry about it. Plus, all of my exams are project based and I kick ass at what I'm studying to do, and I can admit that with a cocky confidence.

"You're literally the worst studier I've ever seen in my life." I chuckle.

"I don't even need this shit. I'm going to be a football player, and that's it. You get to go to school for the thing you love, photography. Why can't I simply attend this school and just focus on football twenty-four seven?"

"Because that's not the way this works, and you know it. Two more years, Stallion, and you can do that all the time. But if you don't pass this class, you can say goodbye to that football field. So you need to study." I give him a stern look.

"Oh, I like you when you're bossy. Come be my teacher, Jimmy." Lincoln tries to grab for me, his voice going all porny.

I kick a leg out at him. "Stop it, you're deflecting. And trying to distract. We've barely been at this an hour. I don't want my boyfriend getting kicked off the team and out of school because he can't remember which grade level sex education is taught in."

"Oh, I'll teach you about sex education, you don't have to worry about that." He all but tackles me until we're lying on top of our textbooks with him in between my thighs.

Lincoln swoops down and kisses me gently, with a teasing smirk, before I can protest any further.

And *damn*, why is he so good at this? I could fail out of Warchester with him as my boyfriend. The distractions are endless.

Boyfriend.

I could have told him no. I could have rejected his offer to be his girlfriend, to be a couple. Right there, on that sidewalk, I could have ended this entire thing and it still would have hurt him. I saw it in Lincoln's eyes as he was pouring his heart out. I could have shattered his feelings and been able to cross off that bucket list item successfully.

But ... I want to be his girlfriend. I want him to be my boyfriend. And if I'm being honest, it has nothing to do with getting revenge for Catherine. Oh, I can lie to myself all day long, convince myself that I'm only bringing him in deeper, hoping he'll fall in love blindly, to then turn around and *really* hurt him on a cellular level.

That's just not true though. When he was standing in front of me, telling me all the ways he cared about me, I was just a girl and he was just a boy. Two people who really have formed something. And it scares the shit out of me.

I'm committed to completing Catherine's list, but how am I going to do that now? When Lincoln means so much to me. When I've realized that he's the only guy I might truly want to be with. Panic has begun to set in.

I could move forward with my plan and potentially break both of our hearts. I could ignore it, betraying Catherine and feeling guilty for the rest of my life. I could come clean to Lincoln, tell him about the list and see his reaction. If I tell the truth about it, he can't be that mad. Right?

Or, I could shove this to the back of my brain and procrastinate doing anything. Living in the moment is so college, and I'm grasping onto that for now.

"Come on, you have to study!" I try to shove at his chest.

"I need a break," he whines, getting off me to sit upright on the bed.

"Fine, but let's have a snack and watch something."

If we had sex right now, we'd surely be done studying for the rest of the night. Lincoln and naked skin is a dangerous combination. Plus, I am hungry.

"Fine. But only if you make that popcorn." He rubs his hands together and grabs my remote.

The kind of popcorn Mom buys and ships to me in a package has become Lincoln's new favorite snack. He ransacks my room and cleans it of all food by the time he stays the night. The guy is a human garbage disposal.

As soon as I hit the buttons on my microwave for the

popcorn setting, I bounce back to the bed and grab the remote from him.

"Nope, my turn. Last week I had to watch an entire tournament of hockey, and that's not even your sport." I stick my tongue out.

Lincoln chuckles. "Sports are sports, babe, I don't discriminate."

I wrinkle my nose. "Babe? No. If you want to be affectionate, it's Jimmy."

The smile on his lips is pressed into my forehead. "You're my Jimmy."

I flip through the documentaries on Netflix, most of the murder ones I already watched. And then a new one catches my eye. "Oh! Let's watch this!"

"Not another one of these," Lincoln complains. "I've seen enough police evidence photos and blood spatter residue to last a lifetime, thanks to you."

The microwave goes off and I hop off the bed, prancing across the room. "Come on, I love this kind of stuff. And you wanted to date me, so you made your bed."

Lincoln's grin is devilish. "And I'd love to unmake yours."

I roll my eyes as I join him with the bowl of popcorn, that he immediately starts to devour. I press play on the documentary, and we're quiet for a few minutes.

An idea strikes me.

"If I asked you to help me bury a body, what would you say?" I ask him, snuggling back into his arms.

I can hear Lincoln thinking. "I would want to know the details. Who was it? Why did you kill them? What's the plan for avoiding detection?"

I scoff. "Jeez, good to know you wouldn't help me in a time of need! You're not supposed to have questions, you're just supposed to be my ride or die. I won't be fucking calling you if I murder someone. You might as well call the cops on me."

He pushes up, scooting so he can look at my face. "No, no, I take it back! I'll be your ride or die. No questions asked. I'll chop up body parts for you, Dexter-style. Put em in bags—"

"No, you already gave your answer. Your help when burying a body comes with strings attached, or questions that is. You've made your loyalty clear." I hold a hand up, teasing him.

"I'd do anything for you, Henley." Lincoln's tone is more serious, all the banter we've been swapping back and forth over the last minute all but gone.

My heart does a nosedive straight to my feet. Because I can tell he really meant that.

And now that I'm stuck between a rock, Lincoln, a hard place, and Catherine's list ... what would I do for him?

Would I be willing to choose him over the best friend I ever had?

LINCOLN

She's up there, in the stands.

My first game as a starter, and my girl is in the stands. Who knew I'd ever be saying the words, "my girl." Certainly not me. Especially when it came to football season.

I've always been the kind of man who thought that having a woman in my life, that dating, would be a distraction. Love was just for suckers, even if girls were fun, and I wouldn't be the kind of person to fall into it without control over my internal organs.

Except now, I'm exactly that person. My nerves are rife with adrenaline just knowing that Henley is going to be watching me start my first game for Warchester. And bringing her here, to California where the game is going to be played, it's a big deal. Only players with serious girlfriends, or sometimes even wives, do that. But I knew, when I got the call from Coach that I'd be starting, that I wanted Henley there with me. She was my support system, and even though we'd only been seeing each other for a couple of months, and dating officially even less than that, she was quickly becoming my everything.

If I'm telling the truth, I'm in love with Henley. Not that I can say that to her yet. It'll freak her the fuck out, so badly that she'll go running to some place I probably won't be able to find her.

"Kolb, I want to see precision tonight." Coach points his finger at me on the sidelines, and I jump up and down, like I'm preparing to go into a cage and slaughter my opponent.

I'd won the last three games as the second half starter and had outshined the junior quarterback by a mile. I worked hard at practice, stayed late, got up early to go to the weight room, and supported my teammates as much as I could. It was nothing against their former starter, but this was my time.

The national anthem begins to play, and my blood courses through my ears. I was destined for this, made to be here in this moment. And made to excel beyond this. I'm so amped up, it feels like my bones could jump out of my body with just the smallest jostle.

Before I listen to Coach, before I march out onto that field to do battle with my guys, I glance up. Fifty yard line, eight rows back. I know that's where she is because I got her the tickets, wanted her right in my sight line.

Henley's eyes are glued to mine, the surety in them so fierce that it makes me even cockier than I was coming into this. I'm going to win this. For my team, for me. *For her.*

She gives me a single nod, and I give it right back, knowing that whatever happens, I'm coming home to her later.

How is it that the concerns I always used to have seem less worrisome, now that I have her? It's like the stress I used to feel, or the problems I'd create, they've just dissipated now that I have someone I love more than myself. Is that what all the fuss is about? Is that why men have gone to war over this, why couples have walked through fire just to be together?

Because I'd do both of those for Henley.

The captains walk out for the coin toss, and I'm not one of them. Understandable, as I'm only a freshman, but I plan to be walking to midfield soon enough to claim heads or tails. I'm the quarterback now, and I plan to be the leader of this team, even if I'm the youngest guy on the roster.

And then it's time. Time for me to march out onto the field, command my troops, and execute plays. I was born for this, I've been working my entire life to get here.

Within the first five minutes, we've scored two touchdowns. One rushing and one with me at the helm, throwing a gorgeous sixty-yard pass to one of my wide receivers.

Come the two-minute warning, Warchester is winning fifty-five to seventeen.

As I run off the field when the final whistle blows, teammates clapping my back and coaches yelling in my ear that I'm a goddamn genius, there is only one set of eyes I search for.

When I find them, I glimpse tears. Henley is crying *for me*. They're running down her face in happy little rivulets, and my heart beats so hard against my rib cage that I'm sure it'll burst free.

It's at this moment that I know, even if she isn't saying it, that she loves me, too.

"I don't think I can do this."

The instructor pulls the strap at my leg, essentially cutting off my circulation while also giving me some sort of weird, sexual adult diaper. The harness would highlight any man's package, but on a woman, it's just digging into places I never wanted to have something dug into.

"You're the one who 'promised' her friend. And now we're here, so you can't chicken out." Lincoln's smile is on full megawatt brightness, and he seems to welcome the idea of death we're about to invite.

Meanwhile, his package *is* highlighted ... and looks more enormous than ever. How is it fair that I have the biggest camel toe of my life, and he looks like some boner god as the rest of the females standing on this bridge eye his cock through his basketball shorts.

We're standing at the top of the Bridge to Nowhere in El Segundo, California, helmets on and eyes glued to the rocks hundreds of feet below. And for the first time since I was given this list by a dying Catherine, I am questioning one of the items on it. It wasn't dying my perfectly blond hair or camping in a goddamn tent. It wasn't even tricking her ex-boyfriend into loving me and then breaking his heart. No, I had no problem with those questionable tasks.

Well, at least not until I was falling head first in love with the ex-boyfriend. Now it's a damn problem but it wasn't in the beginning.

No, it's bungee jumping that's got me shook, and now I'm wondering what the hell Catherine was thinking when she put this on here.

When Lincoln asked if I'd accompany him to his game out here, I looked up one of the only certified bungee jumping places in the continental US. It's about an hour from the site of the stadium he won the game at last night, and since we had an extra day out here before having to return to Warchester for classes, we decided to come out here. I'd told him that a friend, the same one I promised I'd go camping, had influenced me. He hadn't pushed, which I was thankful for.

"Yeah, but I don't think I can do this." I wriggle myself, not sure how I'm going to get free of this bungee.

Especially when I'm strapped to my boyfriend.

Lincoln insisted on doing a jump together; he said he'd like to feel my boobs pressed against him if he was about to die. Not to mention, he could get in serious trouble from his coaches if they found out we were doing this. So, I capitulated, since I was the one who asked him to come do this in the first place.

"Too bad. 'Cause we're up." He shimmies us so that I have to follow, since I'm strapped to his body.

I will say, I got some beautiful photos of other people plummeting to their deaths. Of course, I'd brought my camera, never one to pass up a unique situation to photograph. While Lincoln and I were waiting for our scheduled time slot, I shot some of the other jumpers. The material was really great, and I knew that it would really impress Kyle, my photography professor.

He'd become somewhat of a mentor throughout the semester and was even talking about helping me nab an internship at one of the prestigious magazines he had affiliations at.

But apparently, I was going to risk all that to plummet to *my own* death.

We're helped up onto the jumping ledge by the professionals who have already schooled us in how to fall, how to dangle, and all the other safety stuff we had to take in the pre-jump course. Which was only thirty minutes ago. How I'm supposed to prevent myself from serious brain injury when I was only taught how to do so less than an hour ago is beyond me.

I close my eyes as they count us down, every limb stricken with paralyzing fear.

"You're going to do this. It's going to be incredible," Lincoln whispers in my ear and places a kiss over my lobe.

It distracts me just enough that I don't see it coming when he tips us over the edge. A blood-curdling scream leaves my throat as we fall, the freeness of it almost eclipsing the sheer terror. Lincoln is yelling and laughing all at the same time, and it's too intense, so I shut my eyes.

I think of Catherine, picture her face. She's smiling, one of her effervescent, blissful grins that always made me giggle just a bit. She would have been terrified of this, but after the initial fear seized her, she would have loved this.

So, I focus on that. I hold tight to Lincoln, open my eyes and stare at the landscape around us as we fall. I wish I could capture this with my camera; I wish that Catherine could have seen this for herself.

Even though I know this is mere seconds, the fall seems like hours. The canyon and the water seem to stop, our bodies going in slow motion, and I press my cheek against the boy I'm not only falling with, but falling for.

Once I let go of the fear and allow the tranquilness of this to set in, my bones relax and complete calm settles over my body. When the tether hits its restraint as we hit the bottom of the rope, I'm not even nervous for the recoil.

No, I welcome it, laughing like a fool as we bounce back and forth, our bodies flying this way and that.

And when we finally come to a stop, hanging together like bats, our hands almost able to touch the water below, I look at Lincoln.

His lips come over mine, and the urgent kiss sweeps my body into a flurry of goose bumps.

"That was ..." He trails off, wonder lighting up his face.

"I know." I nod, knowing exactly the words he can't say.

As we're getting unhooked from our harnesses, I feel Lincoln's eyes roaming over my body. My nipples harden, and I'm panting. I could blame it on the whole cheating death thing, but I know what this is.

I want to fuck the life out of him, and I want to return the favor.

Something about the adrenaline of it, the raw feeling of almost dying but surviving the fall, it gets to you. I feel like my whole body is vibrating, operating on some other level, and the only thing I want to do is shed all of my clothes and have Lincoln bury himself inside me.

By the way he's squeezing my hand, I know he's about to whip out his cock and thrust it at me. We're both turned on to the highest degree, our bodies pinging electric currents off each other on the maximum setting of desire.

I can barely keep my hands off of Lincoln in the rented car we drove out here. My lips are on his neck, his fingers dance across my covered thighs, and he moves one of my hands to feel the rigid swell of his cock through his shorts.

"If you don't stop, I'm going to have to pull this car over right here and fuck you in the back seat," Lincoln growls.

"So get us to the hotel faster." I moan, knowing we're just minutes away.

My blood pulses in my ears, and it feels like my heart is about to go into cardiac arrest.

Thank God we checked into the hotel before going to the bridge, because it means we can bypass the lobby and fumble through the side entrance as we kiss. Being that it's the middle of the day, we're lucky no one comes into the hall as Lincoln stumbles over unlocking the door, with my hands nearly down his pants.

It all moves so fast from there.

His hands on my breasts, pulling at my clothes.

My moans filling his mouth as our tongues twine.

Frantic, eating up every part of each other's skin we can taste.

No words are needed right now; we're acting on instinct, pure and primal. Neither of us is prey, and neither of us is the hunter. We're both equal parts in this dance for pleasure. For intimacy.

To feel alive.

We don't even make it to the bed, Lincoln simply hoists me up as soon as we're naked and slides into me. My back connects with the wall, all of his strength holding me there as he joins us.

In his eyes, one green and one blue, I see nothing but flames. Carnal desire, which must mirror my expression. My fingers dig into his shoulder blades, and I surrender myself to the glorious assault he's laying to my body. All I can do is hang on, allow Lincoln to build my climax higher and higher as he thrusts.

We come together in an ovation of haggard breath and whispered curses.

And I've never felt more alive.

L ater, when we're lying naked and entwined in the hotel room bed, something crosses my mind.

"This scar? The one I told you was from football? I lied." My voice is quiet in the dark of the room.

Henley's fingers trail down my scar, tickling my stomach as she goes. She's quiet, not interrupting me but giving me the space to tell her the truth.

"The truth is ... this scar is from when doctors took a bunch of tumors out of my body when I was a kid." I press a kiss to the crown of her head, glad she isn't looking at me in the eye.

The sex we just had was so intense, as if it altered the face of the earth. Or maybe it just altered the face of my earth. That's what Henley seems to do, and I'm not sure how I grew up just a town over from her and never felt her presence. If this was the girl I was meant to be with, it seemed like I'd been biding my time for an awfully *long* time.

And even though she's still tight-lipped about a lot of stuff in her past, I wanted to share all of my secrets with her. Not that this was a secret, per se, but I rarely shared this part of my life with anyone else. It felt more intimate, more personal than sharing the stuff about my cousins.

I liked to assume, and have other people assume, that I have no weaknesses. There was nothing that could take me down. But this scar, and the explanation behind it, proved that there were things that could completely pull me out of the game, not to mention life.

"Tumors?" I feel Henley's body go rigid. Her hand stops stroking the scar.

I nod, though she can't see the motion. "When I was eight, I was diagnosed with leukemia. I came home from school one day with a rash and a fever of about a hundred and four. My parents rushed me to the hospital. Thank God they did, because if they'd treated it like a cold, who knows what would have happened."

There were points back then, glimpses of what I can remember, where the pain was so bad that I thought I was going to die. As a kid, you don't fully grasp that. Death doesn't carry the connotation it does now that I'm an adult. I knew it was scary; I knew that all the procedures were painful, but I didn't fully understand just how fragile my life was in that year.

"You had cancer?" Her voice is a whisper, and I'm pretty sure I hear tears swirling in her tone.

"Yes. I spent almost a year in and out of hospitals. They started with the surgery, removing as many of the tumors as they could. That's what left this scar." I trail my hand down it, and Henley's fingers follow.

I continue, wanting the whole truth between us. "Then it was onto chemo treatments, radiation, blood infusions, special diets. I missed almost an entire year of school, and could barely do anything after treatment. It took me a while after I was deemed in remission to even summon the energy to be a kid."

Now, Henley looks up at me, and there is so much sadness in her face. "I can't even begin to imagine ..."

Gulping, I nod. "I know. It was a really tough thing, and I don't think I understood the gravity of it until much later. It's why I don't talk about it a lot. It's like a jinx, if I talk about it, maybe it will come back. I never want to have to fight that battle again."

"Not a lot of people know about this." Henley says it like a statement, though I know it's a question.

"Showing weakness is not one of my strong suits. I'm supposed to be this legend, this unbreakable captain of my sport. What would they say if they knew I was the kid in elementary school with cancer? The dying child who had all the fundraisers thrown for him? I don't want them to look at me like that."

"But you told me." Again, not a statement.

My hand brushes down her cheek. "Because I want you to know everything about me. I want to give you all of me. And I want you to feel comfortable, when you're ready, to do the same. I see the things you hold back haunting your eyes. I want to be your everything, just like you are to me now."

Though our day started off in a flurry of action-packed adrenaline, it was ending with tenderness.

In this quiet hotel room, with the dim lamp illuminating just one corner of the place, I was all but telling Henley that I was in love with her.

And hoping that soon, she'd be able to tell me she felt the same way.

It just so happens that the hearing I'm supposed to testify at regarding Tyla and Brant's custody falls over Thanksgiving break.

Conveniently, I'm already home. And even more crucial, it means that I'll have Henley close by since she lives a town over. Of course, I have my parents and my brother, who came home to testify as well, but something about hugging Henley after coming off that stand makes my uneasy soul rest somewhat easier.

"You'll be just outside the doors?" I ask, nodding like my answer will come out of her lips.

Henley holds my hands in both of hers. "I'll be right here. You don't have to be nervous, you're Lincoln freaking Kolb. You've got this."

I'm pissed she isn't allowed to come in, but for the sake of the children, this is a closed hearing. I guess that's good, in part, because my Aunt Cheryl can't parade her band of floozy friends in to intimidate us, like that would work, or throw off Tyla and Brant, which is so fucking selfish within itself but something I'd never put past her.

I wrap an arm around her shoulder, pull her into me so I can kiss her. "You really know how to pump a guy up."

"Eh, it's easy when his ego is already so inflated." She winks at me.

Leave it to my girl to use jokes at a time like this. She knows it's exactly what I need, and it's why I'm so fucking glad she's here.

I'm about to try to go slay a dragon. My aunt Cheryl has been a toxic drug in the lives of her children, one we've been trying to rid them of for years. With mine and Chase's testimony, we'll move the custody case just a little further along in our favor.

Someone pops their head out of the room, calling the Kolb family inside.

My brows knit together as I study Henley. "This is it."

"You're going to do good by those kids. They love you like hell. Go love them back."

"You know I do." I squeeze her hand before I turn, walking into the courtroom with the rest of my family.

Luckily, Tyla and Brant get to wait in a different holding room with a supervised agent while we're all grilled in this courtroom. They don't need to hear me bad mouth their mother, even if it's true. They're children, they won't understand. And they'll appreciate what I'm doing when they're older. When they realize just how much better off they are with my parents as their guardians.

"I just want to remind you all that I love you, and I'm proud of you. Whatever happens after today, we all tried our hardest and it doesn't mean we love Tyla and Brant any less."

Dad is basically choking on tears, and we all take a moment to compose ourselves. Shortly after we settle at our table, Cheryl walks in—looking like a mess. She's in a fire engine red dress that's three sizes too tight and four inches too short. Her hair looks like a rat's nest, and even from ten feet away, I can smell the cigarettes and booze on her.

Her boyfriend trails behind her, in jeans and a T-shirt, while the rest of my family has dressed in our nicest suits and clothing to come fight for these kids. If this doesn't outright convince them, our testimony should.

When the judge comes into chambers, we all stand as instructed, and then sit through her opening remarks about the case. She asks some questions of the social workers who have been working on the kids' case since it came about two years ago, and then it's time for my testimony.

"Mr. Lincoln Kolb, please come to the stand," the judge requests.

This isn't a trial, so no lawyers are here to cross examine me. Just the judge, who is going to fire questions at me about our home, my childhood, the state of the children's mindsets, and why I believe that we can give them the best and most loving home. I've already been coached about how this will go, and I wish I could relay that to my nerves, but they practically jumping out of my skin.

This is weightier than any game I've ever played in. Right now, none of that matters. This is about family, and that's the most important thing in life.

"Thank you for being here today, Lincoln." The judge smiles at me, and I know she's trying to make me feel comfortable.

I won't be lulled into a false sense of security though. I'm staying sharp. I have to. "Of course. I'd do anything for Tyla and Brant."

She nods. "So tell me a little bit about your relationship with your cousins."

A softball, right off the bat, and I go into detail about how incredible our family unit has become since they came into it. I tell her about the football practices I used to drive Brant to before I went to college. How Tyla and I liked to make Friday night dinner for everyone. I tell her about the vacation to Disney World we took last summer, and the bedtime routine my parents set up for the little ones that Chase and I participate in every time we're home; bath, book, or seven, and bed. I try to tell the judge every little facet and fact about my cousins' lives with us, so that it's undeniable my parents should have custody.

"And Lincoln, tell me, what have you witnessed when your cousins come home from a visit with their mother?" the judge asks.

"They're scattered, and I can tell that their emotions are all over the place. Brant is too quiet, Tyla looks like she might cry for about a day and a half after every visit. They don't sleep well, their eating schedules are off, and it takes almost a week for them to become their happy, fun loving selves again. I'm not sure what happens at those visits, I can't speak to it, but I personally never want to see those kids in that state again."

I look across to Aunt Cheryl, who is scowling. Her boyfriend is smiling like the devil himself, his broken and golden teeth absolutely disgusting.

"Why do you believe your parents and their home would be a better fit?"

"Because we all love them so much. We want to give them the best life possible, even if that means sacrificing something for ourselves. My brother and I, we're out of the house now. This was supposed to be my parents' time to live out their own dreams. Be empty nesters. Go on wine tours or whatever it is people do who are close to retirement."

The judge chuckles, as do some people in the courtroom.

I go on. "But they've chosen to take on the responsibility to raise these kids. Because that's what you do for family, for people you love. My parents, and my brother and me, we want to give Tyla and Brant the best life they can possibly have. And I believe that's with our family."

"And if someone had come and tried to remove you from your parents' home, how would you have reacted?"

It takes me a minute to breathe down the anger this question evokes. I know what the judge is trying to get at, but I won't be baited.

"I know how important having a relationship with your parents is. The ones who gave life to you, who raised you, who can tell you stories about your history and make memories with you. I know, because I have that. My parents are incredible. I also know that there are people out there who aren't fit or qualified in any sense of the word to be that to their children. If they put themselves before their children, put them in dangerous situations, do anything to put their child in a place of disadvantage or harm, they shouldn't be able to make those memories with their children. I believe this about my aunt Cheryl. She should not have the privilege of caring for her children when she cannot make the sacrifices to do so."

I swear, you can hear a pin drop. I'm only focused on the judge, staring at her so I make my point known.

After a few more questions, mostly evidentiary or research based ones, I'm allowed to step down from the stand. Chase is called up shortly after, and asked mostly the same questions. Cheryl testifies and barely makes a case for why she'd be fit to raise eggs from the grocery store, let alone children.

And then it's over. We're told that the judge will deliberate, that the children will remain in my parents' temporary custody until she's made her decision.

We all walk out of the courtroom together, hugging, saying a silent prayer that we did enough to bring Tyla and Brant home for good.

Henley is sitting on a bench opposite the doors, waiting just like she said she'd be.

Without hesitation, I walk toward her, hauling her up and into my arms. In just a few months, she has become my rock. Just holding her after that emotional turmoil makes me feel immensely better.

So I whisper in her ear, "I can't imagine being without you."

We drive back to Warchester an hour after having dinner with the Kolb family.

Lincoln is mostly silent, and I see him literally chewing his lip as he chews over all the thoughts in his head. I left him be, choosing a good mix of music as the sun set past the windshield. He did hold my hand the entire drive though, and the connection let me know that he wasn't upset.

Just preoccupied.

I understood that, because I was too. Over the last week, I've had so much to think over that it all rattles around in my head. Going home with Lincoln, seeing him so shaken about the custody case, the way he looked at me after we bungee jumped ...

And then the confession he let loose as we lay in that hotel room.

I don't how to reconcile my feelings for Lincoln with feeling guilty about Catherine. This whole thing started as a way to get back at him, and now I'm in love with the guy. How the hell that happened, how I allowed myself to fall ... it was probably inevitable from the start. Not only is Lincoln one of the most charming and gorgeous male specimens I've ever encountered, but I hadn't counted on the fact that he'd *fit* me.

Lincoln surprised the hell out of me by being an equal match. To my wit, to my independence, to my taunting sarcasm. He is interested in me, wants to know about my photography and has supported me since the moment we met.

And on top of everything else, he told me his most intimate secret. His weakness. I know it wasn't easy to reveal to me that he had cancer. How the hell do I fit this into the puzzle? Catherine hated him because he dumped her when she got cancer. We loathed him for what a huge jerk he was, that someone would do that to a person about to battle for their life.

To find out that he went through the same thing, that Lincoln knows firsthand just how horrible and difficult it is to battle that fucking disease ...

How could he do that to her? Did he know how deeply it hurt her? Was he terrified of watching someone else go through that, so he ended it before he had to hold her hand through it?

I wish I could ask him these questions. I wish the answers were as simple as I want them to be. But I know they aren't. Neither is my explanation of what I'm doing.

I want to call off the whole bucket list agenda. I want to be with Lincoln for real, no matter how much guilt churns in my gut thinking about Catherine while admitting that. I want to be there for him in every situation, especially ones like today.

Watching him walk into that courtroom, defend his family, and fight for people he loves.

It's impossible to compare this caring, passionate, extraordinary man with the one Catherine and I demonized in her teenage bedroom. They can't be the same person.

By the time we make it up to my tower, you can feel the exhaustion rolling off of us in waves. Rhiannon is still back home, she'll be at school tomorrow, so Lincoln is spending the night in my dorm room.

"Let's sleep." I usher him in, helping to unbutton his shirt and loosen his tie.

I'm not doing it in a sexual way, but more like a partner caring for her partner. I want to ease his worries, hold him in my arms and bring him whatever comfort I can possibly impart.

"Thank you for being there today." He sighs, toeing off his shoes as I shrug out of the dress I wore to his hometown.

Lincoln pulls my hair out of its clip, and I rub my hands over his bare muscles, trying to soothe away the tension. This is what compassion feels like, this is what contentment feels like.

"I'll always be there when you need me. The only thing I want is to be by your side," I admit.

It's been hard for me to return his romantic or emotional sentiments. I've held myself back, at first because I hated him and then later because I couldn't allow myself to fall in love with him. Distance was my friend, and as long as I could keep my emotions at arm's length, I would be fine.

But I'm done doing that. From this point forward, I'm done with the charade. I loved Catherine like she was my own blood, but in Lincoln I've found the guy I'm sure I'm supposed to be with. It's a daunting fact, and while I feel guilty about keeping him for myself, I know I won't willingly give him up.

Lincoln sighs into me, and I move us to the bed, guiding him as he crawls in and then opens his arms for me.

We lie there for a while, scratching each other gently, caressing skin, exchanging tired, lazy kisses. It's not leading anywhere, but in all of my moments with Lincoln, I've never felt more intimate.

Lincoln is playing with my hair, the signal that he's about to nod off, and my heart warms at how familiar this has become. When you begin to fall for someone, to spend so much time with them, routines are put into place. As a young single person, we're told to fear routine. That change and adventure is what we should seek. But this? I wouldn't trade this for the world.

"I love you," he whispers into the dark.

I almost don't hear it, and for a moment I think I imagine it. But no, I'm not making things up. This man, this frustrating, gorgeous, confident, loving, irresistible man just said he loves me.

Pausing, I try to get my heartbeat under control. I just went from the edge of sleep to slammed into full-on alert mode in two second flat.

But by the time I glance up to look at Lincoln's face, he's fast asleep. His long eyelashes kiss his cheeks, that strong jaw moves slightly with the deep, settled breaths he's taking.

He won't know I said it, which is possibly a good thing for the first time. I need to test the words on my tongue, see how they make me feel.

"I love you, too."

My voice is nothing but a feather, floating over a sleeping Lincoln. But the weight of those words is immense. Both an anvil on my soul and such a relief that I want to cry.

The feeling makes me even more exhausted, and I drift off to sleep in Lincoln's arms.

T he last month of the semester is a race to the finish.

Between football games, classes, trying to carve out time for Henley and everything else, I feel like I'm losing my mind.

Our team was selected to play in one of the bowl game play-offs that lead to the championship, and everyone is feeling the pressure. It's like a powder keg at every practice, we're just wholly ready to light that stadium up come Christmas break. Then, when we win, we'll be in the championship just after New Year's.

This is one of the moments I've been waiting for in my life, and each day that brings me closer just brings me one step toward my destiny.

Finals are literally nonexistent for me, as is my major. Any professor who assumes division one athletes are in college for any other reason besides their sport is in for a rude awakening.

But I finally have one night off, and I reserved it just for Henley. She gave me the key to her dorm room since she was on a shoot that her professor set up for her until a little later. Kyle, her professor, had gotten her onto the set of this epic magazine article, and she was the only student invited. It was a major accomplishment, and she'd learn a ton. My girl had been going on and on about it for weeks, and I was so proud of her.

And I am also in love with her. Weeks ago, I told her so while I drifted off to sleep. I know she thinks I don't remember that, but I do. I haven't brought it up again because I don't think she's ready to say it back, but I just needed her to know. Through all the craziness of our two lives the past month, and beyond it, I wouldn't want anyone by my side but her.

Though I am a tad annoyed, because she lost her remote again and I am stuck in this room with no TV and no sex. I rummage around her bed, thinking it might have fallen in the cracks. And then I search under it, wading through the mountain of shoes she stores under here.

Having no luck, I focus on her desk, which is piled high with photography books and camera supplies. Scanning it, I don't see the remote, so I open the middle drawer, thinking maybe Henley stuck it in here in a moment of not thinking.

My hands blindly fumble, hitting random desk items like a stapler and a box of paper clips, and then touch some rumpled piece of paper. I pull it out, thinking it had to be garbage, until I see what's written on it.

At the top, in clear cursive letters, is written "Catherine O'Mara's Bucket List."

Wait, *what*? Catherine? How the hell ...

I scan the list, looking at the lines crossing most of the items out. Go to Paris, dye her hair, go on a camping trip ...

Wait a minute ...

And then my eyes hit the last one.

Get revenge on Lincoln Kolb.

Just as I read it, my name in that pretty handwriting, the sound of the door opening hits my ears.

"Hey, Stallion, thanks for waiting. I brought us craft services from the set, got you two whole subs they were going to just chuck!" Henley sounds elated, and smug that she scored us free food.

"What the fuck is this?" I ask, turning to her with the list in my hand.

I don't miss the way her eyes literally almost bug out of her head. "That's ... uh ... nothing ... uh ..."

"Bullshit, Henley, don't fucking lie to me. How the hell did you know Catherine O'Mara?"

My world is tumbling off its axis, everything feeling too close and incredibly spaced out all at once. None of this makes sense, and I can't connect thoughts in my head. It's like my synapses refuse to fire because they're just so goddamn confused.

"Why were you snooping around in my drawers?" she demands, which only gets me more irate.

"Oh, no you don't. We're not playing that game. What the fuck is this?" I shake the paper at her while she lunges for it.

Henley looks like a crazed animal, one who is caught between being eaten and jumping off a cliff to her death. She has nowhere to go, no excuse to escape this.

"Catherine was my best friend, we lived on dividing lines between Little Port and Winona Falls. I was there every time she got sick, from the time we were three to up until her death. She was a sister to me. When she started dating you, I'd never seen her more giddy. And then her cancer came back. And you dumped her like she was a piece of trash. So, we started the list. Everything she wanted to do before she died, because we both knew this time it wasn't letting go of her. Getting revenge on you was one of her top priorities, for the way you'd broken her heart. For the way you'd embarrassed her."

Henley is huffing out breaths, her cheeks pink, her eye contact steely. This is the face of grieving, of a girl so angry at the world that she can't contain it. How come I'd never seen this lying underneath the mask she'd used to fool me? I'd never had one inkling.

Suddenly, it all clicks into place. The town she grew up in being right next door to mine. The friend she promised she'd do all those things for. Flashing in my mind is every interaction we've ever shared, and I know now ...

Henley tricked me. She sabotaged me, lured me in like some kind of siren just so she could bring me to my knees.

"This is fucking insane." I breathe, not talking to anyone really but shaking my head as if I'll wake up from this nightmare.

"You dumped her! In the middle of everyone! Knowing she had cancer! What kind of person does that? An asshole. A horrible human being, that's who!" Henley screams, throwing her hands up.

Jesus Christ, she's trying to defend her actions because I dumped a high school girlfriend three weeks into us dating.

"You don't fucking know me!" I shout at her, veins popping in my neck.

Henley gets right up in my face, her cheeks redder than any shade I've ever seen. Even with venom running through my blood, I can appreciate that this girl isn't a fucking chump. She'll jump into the ring with lions, snakes, or otherwise and give them hell. It's probably why I was so fucking attracted to her—why I still am despite her massive betrayal.

"And you don't fucking know me. You think that because I let you inside me, that you know everything there is to know about me? You're a moron, Lincoln. You wouldn't know how to learn about a woman if she wrote a hand-curated fucking list. All there is to understand is her bra size and her favorite sexual position, isn't that the case?"

"Get the fuck out of here with that, Henley. Don't you even fucking dare. Have I not been here every day for you? Walking you home from class, from parties at one in the morning, helping you bungee jump even though you didn't even want to? And yeah, being inside you might be fucking heaven for me, but it's more than that. I told you shit I've never told another girl before. I've said stuff to you that I haven't felt for anyone. I told you I'm in love with you, Henley! Not that you returned the feeling. And now this? Yeah, apparently I don't fucking know you because someone I thought I knew inside and out was just here to fucking dupe me."

I throw my hands up in the air and storm away from her, so hurt that I can't even look at her. I feel like there is a knife jutting out of my back, and at the same time feel like I plunged one through hers. Because if I'm being honest, I kind of feel like I deserved this too.

What I did to Catherine O'Mara was horrible, I know that. I never should have dumped her like that. In fact, I shouldn't have dumped her at all. I was selfish, horny, and looking for a good time with a hot girl. Her illness, and all the issues it brought with it, was not what I wanted for senior year. And the issues it dug up inside me, about my own mortality and my own remission ... it was more than I could handle.

I was a complete asshole to her, and what I did was dirty and wrong. There were so many times I wanted to apologize, to drive over to her house, to tell her that I should have treated her better. That I could have been there for her as a friend, knowing what she was going through.

But I didn't. Because I was a douchebag. And just now, when I thought I was starting to change, when I thought I found the one girl who could make me a better man ...

She turns around and backhands me to the heart. Henley

had double crossed me, fooled me once and then twice without me even realizing it.

Shame on me, because I was the one who fucked up first. But shame on her for being ruthless enough to carry this out.

"What I did to Catherine, it was terrible. She didn't deserve one minute of it, and I'm so fucking sorry for that. She was a wonderful girl. But what you've done? It surpasses all the selfish things I've done in my life. You're a con artist, I'm not even sure I know who is under that mask. I don't think I want to know. I may have been an asshole, but at least I was honest and upfront. I didn't lie and cheat to break someone's heart."

I shake my head in dismay, trying to work my words past the lump in my throat. I'm losing it all right now. The newfound, quiet, softer side of myself I hadn't given room to for many years. A friendship that made me laugh until I was almost pissing my pants. And the girl who I thought I might be with until I was old and gray.

"I didn't know what to do, after I got to know you. I swear, Lincoln, I've been so messed up for weeks." Tears are coming down her face now.

"For weeks? You've been messed up for weeks? How about the almost four months we've been together? How about every single day we've spent with each other? The nights I've spent in your bed, or the weekends you've spent in mine. Jesus Christ, Henley, you really excelled in the whole undercover game, didn't you? Because I never saw this coming. You did it, you got your revenge. Was it worth it?"

Rhiannon walks in the door on the tail end of me telling Henley off. "What the hell is going on?"

"Not now, Rhi—" Henley starts, but I cut her off.

"Your roommate is a fucking liar." I all but slap the piece of paper into Rhiannon's hands. "Feel free to explain, Henley. We're done."

And without waiting for anymore of her traitorous, devious words, I storm out of there.

I guess she fucking did. Got revenge on Lincoln Kolb. Broke my fucking heart.

Thanks to her, I'll never trust a girl with it again.

34

It's been twenty-four hours since my world imploded, and no one I know on this campus will talk to me.

After Lincoln stormed out, Rhiannon took the letter, read it over, and had so many questions that I thought my head would explode.

I explained the entire, dirty thing to her, from the beginning to the end. And when I finished, I saw nothing but hurt in her eyes. The first question out of her mouth was, "Why didn't you think you could talk to me about her? About this? I thought we were friends."

We are. We were. I'm not sure if she'll ever speak to me again, after what I've done. She certainly hasn't in the last day.

Rhiannon basically listened to my side of the story, and the more I told it, the worse it sounded to my own ears. Catherine and I were childish, stuck in teenage drama and made all that more upset by her diagnosis. We almost blamed her getting sick on Lincoln, that's how far our hatred went.

When I stopped talking, stopped answering questions, she said she was so disappointed in me that she couldn't stay in our room. She packed what little she had left to take home for winter break, which started tomorrow ... or today, I guess, and then went to Alden's room for the night.

I have no idea what's going to happen next semester. Here we had this budding friendship, this bond that you can only have with your freshman year roommate. They're your friend by default, and you cling to each other to survive the new adultness of college. Rhiannon was the closest thing I had to Catherine since her death, and now I'd pretty much ruined that.

It all hurt, each gaping wound carving fault lines in my heart.

Lincoln was right, I'm a liar. A cheat. A con artist. And I hadn't even tried to make him see what I'd come to feel for him. Instead, I stood by Catherine, defending her honor to a man who had never been anything but wonderful to me. I screamed at him, called him the worst kind of names, and turned this all around on him.

When I did try to take ownership, my words came up short. They were a copout, and not at all how I really feel inside. I did this to myself, both lost the man I'm in love with and dismantled my own heart. I knew, going in, that the fallout would be messy, but I never expected to feel like this.

This is that can't eat, can't sleep, can't function kind of heartbreak that all the movies and books tell you about. I never actually thought it was real, until Lincoln Kolb came into my life.

I'm in love with him, plain and simple. There is nothing else I want more now than to apologize, to grovel, and to have him come back to me. My entire life, I've been an independent woman. I never needed much in the arena of love, could take care of myself, had my eyes focused solely on my career and my photography.

But now, the only thing I can seem to think about is telling Lincoln how I feel. Apologizing, begging, doing whatever it takes to make up for the pain I've caused.

I've been sitting in this room all day, staring at my cell phone, my laptop, and any other device or mode that Lincoln might be able to contact me on. He's returned none of my attempts to apologize. Not my calls, or texts, or emails, or social media messages.

I can't do this anymore. I know it's been less than a day that my treachery has sunk in, but I'm not going to sit idly by while my relationship goes up in flames. I'm not going to waste another minute not telling Lincoln that I'm in love with him.

Because if I learned anything from Catherine, it's that life is way too fragile, and way too short.

Swiping away the tears that seem to be permanently pouring down my face, I throw on sneakers and a sweatshirt. Taking the tunnel between our two tower dorms at a sprint, my heart leaps into my throat thinking about seeing Lincoln's face in just a few moments. All around me, students carry their bags to their cars or parent's cars, headed home for Christmas or the other various holidays. My parents aren't coming until tonight to pick me up, which luckily gives me the option to apologize to Lincoln.

I bound up the stairs, sneaking onto his floor before the door closes behind a retreating student. Walking to his door, I push my hand into my chest, just above my heart, trying to calm it.

Standing in front of it, I knock. Wait a second. And then knock again.

My heart falls, because I know he's not here. I've missed this shot. It'll be days before I can get to him, *if* I can get to him.

When there is no answer at his door, and the rest of the dorm seems to be silent as a church mouse; I turn to leave.

It's time to go home, back to the house where Catherine and I planned up this whole bucket list, and lick my wounds.

Then, I'll figure out how to win back the man I love.

35

LINCOLN

This should be the game of life.

Well, the game of my life *before* the actual game of my life.

My head should be completely screwed on, focused on nothing other than plays, formations, and throwing the perfect spiral.

Except, as I go into the second quarter with our team trailing the opponent by ten points, all I can think about is the painful throbbing in my chest. I know it's not a real physical pain, there is no medical condition I can attribute to this.

This aching, tearing, muscle being ripped from muscle feeling is what the love gurus call a broken heart. This is what happens when the girl you're in love with betrays you. This is how it feels to fall completely for someone and then have the relationship come to an earth-shattering halt.

Henley, and what she did, is always at the forefront of my mind, and try as I might, I can't push her out.

I found out that Henley Rowan was Catherine's best friend. That they grew up next door to each other in houses that strad-dled the town lines of Little Port and Winona Falls. I assume that I won my spot on that list Catherine made after we broke up, and Henley carried the grudge long after she passed away.

From talking to friends back home, Henley and Catherine were inseparable. How I never knew this is a mystery to me, but it's probably because I was so damn full of myself in high school that I didn't care to find out anything about the girl I was dating. I was a selfish prick, only into looks and parties and who could get me another rung higher on the social ladder.

Catherine O'Mara was beautiful in that girl next door way. She was pretty as a flower on a spring day and had this air about her that just left you wanting more. Our relationship consisted of nothing more than kissing in the hallways of school, hanging out in group settings on Friday night, and sloppily making out at the occasional party. We were boyfriend and girlfriend for all of a month. The whole thing was so juvenile that I honestly didn't think it would be a big deal that I broke up with her.

No, scratch that, I knew it was the wrong thing to do. No, it wasn't actually. I'm so confused I can't think straight.

Breaking up with Catherine was the right thing to do. Our relationship was surface level, and she needed people surrounding her through her cancer battle that would be there for her and not clam up the second she talked about it. With my history, with the fear that illness brought on for me, I knew I couldn't be that for her.

The way I went about it, though? That was so damn wrong. I shouldn't have done it so casually, I should have told her about my own battle with leukemia, and promised to be there as a friend. Humiliating her in front of our lunch table was such a dick move, and I'll regret that for the rest of my life.

I saw the hurt it caused Henley, so I can't even imagine what it did to Catherine. Henley had been irate, and I could tell that all the anger she'd bottled up toward me was finally flowing out.

Her pain and fury were lava, decimating everything in their path.

I should hate her for what she's done, but in a twisted way, I understand it. I hurt the person she loved most, and getting revenge made her feel better about her grief.

It doesn't soothe the hurricane mutilating my heart, though. I lost the only girl I've ever loved, and in a time when I need my rock most, she isn't here. I'm not allowing her to be here. I can't fathom coming back from this, there is no way we can move on.

"Dude, focus!" Janssen shouts at me in the huddle.

The other guys look at him and then back at me. I growl like I might rip his face off. At this point, I'd love to pummel something. Anything.

"I am." My voice is clipped.

"Sure as hell doesn't look like it. We're down by ten and their quarterback has nothing on you. Where the fuck is Lincoln Kolb?" Janssen pokes the bear again.

I have to fist my gloved hands to keep from punching him in the helmet. That would only hurt me more than I already am.

"I'm trying to work with what I'm given. We need to be tighter, offensive line, I need you blocking more," I yell over the noise of the crowd.

"And you need to get her out of your fucking head." Derrick's eyes are pure rage. "She did you dirty, my brother, and there is no sense in letting her mess up your career, too. Forget about her, at least for the next three quarters."

Well, shit. Guess Janssen spilled the beans to everyone about what went down with Henley. He was there, in my dorm room, when I came back from finding that list, and had talked me down after I couldn't stop my hands from shaking.

"That's none of your fucking business." The words sound like a curse.

"Actually, Linc, it is. Because it's fucking up our chances to go win a national championship. We just have this playoff left, and then we're golden. I know you're hurting, but you have to push past it. If not for you, then for us."

Janssen's words are gentler now, and the fog of rage that has clouded my vision for a week raises slightly. I look around the huddle at my teammates. At the men who have put their bodies and brains on the line to help us all play the sport we love. He's right. I'm letting them down. I'm letting my personal shit interfere with the one thing I've always been able to use to tune everything else out.

"I'm sorry. You're right. From this moment on, it's nothing but football. It's nothing but our team. We're going to win this, you understand me?"

As I put one word in front of the other, my own confidence builds. I feel the energy around the circle rising too, the electric zaps moving from one player to the next.

"Hands in." Derrick nods.

We all put our fists together, on the count of three crying Warchester.

In one last fleeting second, I let myself picture Henley's face. Feel the full weight of how much I miss her, love her, hate her. And then, I push it out of my brain.

I had a dream long before I met her, and I wasn't going to let her fucked-up mission screw with my head one more second.

Before I move forward, in the way I truly want to, I have to get right with the one person who always mattered the most.

"Hey, Cat." I smooth my hand over her grave and then pull my arms around me to bolster from the frigid wind.

I've been home for about a week, celebrated Christmas with my family, and I finally feel like I can face her. I've been mulling it over, chewing my nail beds down to the quick, trying to debate what I should do. My mind has been in overdrive, from feeling immense guilt about Lincoln to sadness over what I'd done, to betrayal of Catherine. I'd been a wreck, not sleeping or eating much while I decided how to make amends.

I sit down next to her, almost as if we were sitting on her bed with its pink sparkly comforter. I rest my cheek against the stone bearing her name, and start to talk.

"I did it." My voice breaks, and tears begin to slide down my face. "I completed your bucket list. It only took me about the first semester of college, so I think you'd be proud."

I have to collect myself, gulping in air. Everything about being here fucking sucks. The fact that my best friend is in the ground instead of right in front of me, able to respond to what I'm saying. The fact that she couldn't do this list herself.

And the fact that I may have completed all of her tasks, but while finishing the last one, I broke my own heart in the process.

"The camping sucked, Cat. I don't know why you put that on there. There weren't even any outlets for a blow-dryer, so I don't know what you would have done. And wiping with a leaf? Yeah, no, I'll never be doing that again."

My laugh is full of emotion and unshed tears as I think about Catherine trying to camp. She would have been so gung ho, and then complained the minute she had to sleep on the dirt.

"And bungee jumping? Why? I did it, but I almost peed my pants. I get why you put it on there, though. The rush you get from doing it makes you feel so alive, you can practically see the blood rushing through your veins. I can only imagine how that would have made you feel."

I choke up, because in those last days with her earthside, she talked so much about wanting to feel alive. She was pissed off that she had to give herself over to death, because there was so much left in her that she wanted to do.

"My hair was red for all of a day, but I did it for you. My roommate helped me dye it. Her name is Rhiannon, I know you'd like her. She can be obnoxious, but you would have gotten along great."

I try to think of soft-spoken Catherine putting up with Rhiannon and it makes me grin.

"The last one ... Cat, I did it. It fucking killed me, but I did it. He's hurting, just like you did."

No, worse than you did, I think. But I won't say that to someone who only wanted revenge on the guy who dumped her over cancer.

"I'm in love with him, Catherine," I whisper, putting my hand to my mouth to stop the sob that might erupt.

The wind picks up, leaves curling through the air, and I swear I feel her there.

"I don't know what happened, but somewhere in between hating him for what he did to you and trying to break his heart, mine got so tangled up in the process that it's not even my own anymore. He's incredible, Cat, and I think ... this sounds so fucked up, but I think we were meant to find each other. That's so fucked up, I know. I know you must hate me. God, please don't hate me ..."

My voice cracks, and I break down into sobs. I rest my arms on the top of her gravestone, wishing so badly she could hug me back.

"He never meant to hurt you, he's so sorry he did. But I lost him because of what I did, and now I fear I'll never find someone I love as much as him. I don't want to find someone. I can't explain it, Cat, but he's just ... he's it. I'm scared out of my mind about how much I love him, and at the same time, I want to rip my hair out because I'm the one who fucked it up."

Right about now, she would tell me to stop cursing; my best friend always did try to be prim and proper.

"We were teenagers, Cat, ones with an expiration date. Your life, our friendship, it all felt so much more intense because there was an end point. So we demonized him. When in fact, Lincoln was just a stupid, scared guy terrified of being with someone who reminded him so much of his weakness. What he did was awful, but what I did was worse."

I swallow, my pride and my hurt and my nerves, for this next bit. "I hope you can understand. I hope you can make peace with my decision. I think, in a way, you were maybe meant to bring Lincoln and I together. He was my savior this year, after you left. I love him, Cat, and I'm going to try to make it right. I also love you, I always will."

Resting my cheek against her gravestone, a gust of wind picks up my hair, sending it swirling. Maybe it's her, giving me the comfort I need. Maybe it's my imagination, giving me the peace I've sought since she passed.

Either way, when I get up to leave with one final glance at her name carved into the stone, I feel a sense of completion that I haven't felt in a very long time.

Two and a half weeks later, I arrive in my hometown a national champion.

There are banners on the storefronts on Main Street, heralding me as their hero. When I run into a few parents of kids I went to high school with, they clap me on the back and tell me how proud of me they are. The local radio station wants me to come in and do an interview, talk about how I won the game for Warchester on a Hail Mary pass.

I should feel on top of the world. This was the dream, I should have finally solidified my ego as a demigod. I'd gotten my national championship ring, and my name was even more on the radar when it came to professional football now.

Except ...

I can't seem to feel anything past a fleeting spark of joy. Nothing. Nada. The team and I went out to party for three days straight after our win, and all I did was get mind-numbingly drunk each night and pass out in a blissful state of blackness. I didn't celebrate so much as consume enough alcohol to put myself to sleep.

There is nothing that excites me, no one I can talk to that will boost my mood.

The one person I want to see, the only one I should stay away from, is the one person I'm actively seeking out.

I haven't returned Henley's calls, texts, messages, or anything else in almost a month. It's nearly the end of winter break, after all the holidays and all of my games are done, and I've done nothing but bum around in my hometown. And try to get my head straight.

During our playing time, I didn't allow myself to think about Henley or our fucked-up situation. I stayed true to my team-mates, obeying Janssen when he said to put her out of my head for the good of our squad.

But after?

I hunkered down in my childhood bedroom and just ... thought.

I considered so many things. How I felt about Henley before I knew about the bucket list. The weight of what I'd done to Catherine. What Henley must have been feeling after Catherine's death. If I could ever trust her again.

I've had enough time and distance to really mull things over, to see my part in things, and also let go of some of the anger. Now, I want answers straight from the horse's mouth. I'm not the kind of guy to leave things unsettled, especially since I'm in love with Henley, and she's the only woman I've ever been in love with.

Navigating my car to the town limits of Winona Falls, I drive slowly past Catherine's house. There, on the corner of the property, I see the sign that reads "Welcome to Little Port." And on the other side is a two-story, brick and white-shingled house. I know it's the Rowan home, because I've asked around and because Henley already told me that she and Catherine were neighbors.

Slowing to a stop in the street, I put the car in park and stare at the house for a moment. This conversation could go so many ways. It could make me angrier, separating me from Henley even further. I could understand her point of view and see light at the end of the tunnel. One thing I knew for sure was that this feeling in my chest, the one that was squeezing my heart like a vise, wasn't going away.

All of my nerves are on high alert as I walk to the door, and I hope to God that her parents don't answer. I have no idea if they know about me at all, and this sure isn't the time to be introduced.

I ring the doorbell with a shaking finger and wait. Almost a minute later, it opens, revealing Henley in those mouth-watering yoga pants she loves to wear. Her hair is piled on top of her head, her skin free of makeup, and those chocolate eyes are wide with surprise.

I hate that my first instinct is to pull her into me and taste her skin. I have to actively fight that response, because my God does she look like a sight for sore eyes.

"Lincoln?" Her voice is pure shock.

"Hi." I try to keep my tone even. "I ... want to talk."

I watch as Henley audibly gulps, her nerves evident in her expression. "Of course, come on."

She invites me inside, and her house isn't at all what I imagined. Henley's side of the dorm room is a modern, black and white landscape that makes you feel both classy and comforted at the same time. Clearly, this is her parent's house, because the down-to-earth farmhouse style and collectable chicken figurines all over the bookcase is totally not Henley.

"I can't believe you're here," she says, standing awkwardly in the middle of the living room.

Though she doesn't invite me to sit, I cross to one of the

couches. I can't stand here and weirdly have this conversation. Plus, we might be here for a while.

I crack my knuckles, looking down at my fist in my lap, as I think of how to begin.

"It took me a long time to want to talk to you. I was too angry, too blindsided. I had other shit going on for me, and I didn't need you interfering with that."

When I look up, Henley looks stricken. Good, she should feel that way. I meant it, that I didn't need our shit in my head while I was trying to take my team to victory.

"I also couldn't believe you'd let me tell you I loved you, knowing the entire thing was a sham."

The amount of shock I'd felt when I found that list, it still hadn't dissipated. I'm still thoroughly surprised that Henley managed to do this, that the plan to make me fall in love with her was this intricate.

"I can't believe that the first real relationship I had, the one I wanted to commit to ... it was a lie."

She shakes her head frantically. "It wasn't a lie though, Lincoln. Maybe it was at the beginning, but over time it changed. I changed. It became less about Catherine and more about my feelings for you. I wasn't going to go through with it. Before you found that list, I was already going to destroy it. I was going to be with you. I went back and forth for so long about whether or not to tell you, but the thought of losing you terrified me. Turns out, in the end, I did anyway."

"Why did you do it?" I have to look in her in the eye, though I guess I'm a poor judge of if she's lying or not.

Henley sighs, and when she looks at me, there are tears in her eyes. "Because Catherine asked me too. And when your best friend dies at the age of eighteen, you do what they've requested. She built you up so much in my head, made you this unforgivable character. She was in so much pain those last months, and I put that on you. Looking back, examining the whole thing, it was completely unjustified. You were a shitty teenage boy, but you barely broke her heart. The two of us, Cat and I, we were pissed at the world. It's not fair that she's gone. So I thought, if I kept up my end of the bargain, that in the end, it would give me a sense of relief to fulfill her bucket list. God, I was so wrong, Lincoln. I knew it from the start, obviously, that I shouldn't do it. But then, I got to know you. I kissed you, I laughed with you. At a certain point—"

I cut her off, not ready to hear about all of her feelings. I couldn't crumble, not yet. "Were you ever going to tell me?"

Henley waits a beat, breathes. "Honestly, I'm not sure. By the point I knew I wasn't in this for revenge anymore, I was so scared to do anything. We were amazing, I didn't want to ruin that. And by the time I knew I was in love with you, I couldn't risk losing you by telling you the truth."

I was going to give him more time, let the dust settle until we got back to Warchester.

Turns out, I didn't need to wait. Lincoln had come to me, though it wasn't for the tearful reunion I'd been dreaming and wishing for every night when I closed my eyes to sleep. He was here for answers, explanations. The sorrow in his eyes every time he looks at me is heart wrenching, and I fear that it'll remain there each time we see each other from now on.

"You what?" His voice is quiet.

I know what he's asking. "I love you. I should have said it so long ago, back before the night you even whispered it before you fell asleep. But I-I didn't know what to do. I felt trapped between loving my best friend and loving you. Between honoring her and moving forward with the only guy I've ever felt this right about. What should I have done? Please, just tell me, because I wish I had a time machine so I could go back and do it."

I hear it, the begging in my voice, the pleading. The tears that have been coming frequently since I've been home on break don't fail me now, and I swipe angrily at them. Lincoln doesn't deserve for me to break down. I'm the one who did this to us.

"You're still grieving," he says, more an observation than a question.

But I need to explain. "*God*, yes. I think about her every day. How unfair it is that she's not here. How fucking terrible cancer is. I think about what she'd be studying, the friends she'd make. You know Warchester was her first choice? I wonder where we'd be in ten years, if she'd have children. I, and everyone who loved her, will never know. We don't get to know, and that's what kills me. Some days, I can't stand being here while she's not."

My heart breaks right open, the severe cracks it in giving way.

Lincoln's expression gives way from its stony appearance to a smidge of empathy. "She was a really great girl."

I nod, trying to swallow the emotion in my throat. "She was. But, in this case, we were both so terribly wrong. I'm so sorry, Lincoln. I need to tell you a lot of things, but an apology should come first. What I did was horrible. I hurt you, and I'll never be able to fully forgive myself for it."

"Would you do it all over again?" he asks, breathless.

I shrug. "It got me to you, one way or another. I don't think I would have taken that chance if it weren't for Cat's bucket list, no matter my intention. Maybe this is what was meant to happen."

"I don't know if I can ever trust you again. When I found that list, fuck, Henley. It felt like my world was going up in flames. I was in love with you. Hell, I'm still in love with you. I can't seem to turn it off, no matter how much it feels like you lodged a knife in my back. One second, I'm resolved with not being with you, and the next, I want to run straight back to you."

"I love you." I walk to him, kneeling down so that I can hold his face in my hands. "I've been in love with you for a while now, and you deserve to know that. You have every right to hate me, to not get past this. But I need to tell you before I can't again, that you're the perfect man to me, Lincoln. You're kind in a way that a lot of people aren't, you don't need to show it but you act on it. You're so confident in everything you do, sometimes in a way that is so annoying but endearing, nonetheless. When you look at me, I feel like the best version of myself. It scares me how much I care about you. You're funny, damn funny, even though I know it's only going to your head when I say that. And when I fall asleep in your arms, it's the one place on earth I feel fully complete. I'm not saying this is going to be easy, it'll probably be really fucking hard. You won't trust me, I'll retreat, we'll fight. But I want this, Lincoln. I want you. I'll do whatever it takes. Please, give me one last shot."

I know I'm begging, that I look weak and it goes against everything I stand for. I'm a strong woman, one who doesn't need anyone else. But I know when I'm in the wrong, and I can own up to that. Especially if it means fighting for a love that fills me up like no other.

Lincoln covers my hands with his, where they rest on his cheeks, and closes his eyes.

"Despite it all, I still love you. You're infuriating and I hate you more right now than I love you, but I can't stand feeling like this anymore. I haven't stopped thinking about you since I stormed out of your dorm room. You're hellfire and unbendable, but I fucking love that. I've never felt more myself than when I'm with you."

He doesn't agree to anything, instead, we just pause, our lips just millimeters apart, while he searches my face.

"I can't imagine the pain you've gone through. I don't know what I'd do if I lost someone that close to me. Just losing you for a few weeks, I'm going insane. It seems so easy, to just go right back. To forget all of this. But we can't do that. What happened ... it changes this. But I also don't want to walk away. I can't walk away."

"It guts me that I hurt you." Lincoln thumbs away a tear that falls down my cheek.

"I want you, Jimmy. Only you. We'll figure it out. No, it won't be easy. But nothing we truly want ever is."

"I love you, Lincoln."

I barely get the words out before our lips collide, meeting in such a passionate kiss that I nearly bowl over. I've been waiting endless days and nights to feel his mouth on mine again, to feel the redemption of his caress. We're not out of the woods, not by a mile, but he's here. He wants to try.

He loves me.

That's all I can ask for. Now, it's my turn to prove just how much he means to me.

U sing the key, I open the dorm room door.

"Well, just let yourself in, why don't you?"

Her voice is teasing, and Henley is facing away from me, making her bed with freshly washed sheets, as I come into the room.

"You're the one who gave me the key," I say, coming up behind her.

I should help her, reach a hand in and grab a corner to make this process faster, but instead, I latch my hands to her hips, admiring the ass I can't wait to see bare and beneath me.

"You could help, you know." I don't even have to see her face to know she's rolling her eyes.

"But this is so much more fun." My lips find the sensitive spot on her neck.

It's been about ten days since we talked at her house, and in that time we've invested in conversations. We've had big ones, small ones. Ones that have ended in tears, others that have ended in needing space, and some that end up with me inside her, pummeling away both of our feelings. Ten days does not make up for all the mistrust she created, but we're on our way to healing. We're in a much better place than we were, and our bond is getting stronger every day.

"Thanks for coming over. It really means a lot." Henley's voice and expression are sincere when she turns to me.

I circle my arms around her, breathing in her scent and feeling complete. It's our first night back at Warchester, the eve of the start of the second semester, and I wouldn't want to be anywhere but with her.

She and Rhiannon still have some issues to iron out, but at least she gave us the night to ourselves and headed to Alden's. They're going to be okay, just like my friends will have to be now that I've chosen to get back together with Henley. Janssen is still skeptical, and told me he's going to make her take a lie detector test weekly, but I know he's just looking out for me.

"Is that bed almost ready? I want to destroy it."

We've had to sneak around while at home, in basements and our cars, while trying to have sex. It was kind of hot, having to revert back to high school ways, but having our own beds in our own private dorms is one hundred times better.

"Hold your horses. I ordered us calzones, buffalo chicken, your favorite."

I rub my hands together. "I like this Henley apology tour. I could get used to this."

She scowls, but I see the uncertainty in her eyes. Every time I make a comment like that, she doubts herself. I don't mean to make her do it, but I also want us not to forget how we got here.

"Hey, I love you, you know that?" I nod and press my forehead to hers.

She gulps. "I love you, too."

"So, what do we do until the calzones get here?" I wink.

Henley pushes away from me. "Well, you could do that advanced reading for class that I know you didn't do."

"Come on, don't get on me about studying yet," I whine.

"What am I going to do with no football for another six months?"

"Actually focus on school?" Henley chuckles.

I did have one thing to look forward to.

"Well, we do get to go home for Tyla and Brant's adoption."

My parents finally got word from the court. After all the judge's considerations, and the evidence the social workers presented, she is giving my parents full legal custody of Tyla and Brant. After all the strife, all the heartache, the court battles and the pain the kids have had to go through, they're finally coming home. To the right home.

Their adoption hearing is at the end of the month, though it's just a technicality at this point. And my parents are having a huge party afterward, to celebrate something we've been holding back being happy about for years.

Of course, it doesn't mean Cheryl is completely out of the picture. She'll still be able to petition for visits, but my parents will have much more control over them now. She'll have to submit for drug tests and prove she's living in a safe environment. Which means, no boyfriends with rap sheets on the premises. If she wants to have a relationship with her children, she'll try to make those things a priority.

But for now, we don't have to worry about it. Because they're with us. Permanently.

And I'm with Henley, permanently. We still have days of doubting, ones where she is distant and grieving, and others where I'm sullen and can't get the past out of my head.

But this is the girl I've chosen to love. No, in reality, I never had any choice.

Henley Rowan came into my life like a meteor, destroying anything that came before her and changing the landscape of my life forever after.

And I wouldn't have it any other way.

EPILOGUE
HENLEY

Two Years Later

"I think there is enough man meat in this room to feed an entire barbecue of hungry jersey chasers."

My lips are at Lincoln's ear, and my boyfriend chuckles, patting my knee over the skin-hugging black dress I have on. After all, I have to look sexy as fuck to ward away those chasers, especially after tonight.

You know, when my man goes number one in the draft.

"Why are you worrying about man meat, you've got yours right here." His eyebrow spikes, those heterochromatic eyes twinkling with sarcasm.

"Just gotta protect what's mine. You think I should go all Rachel McAdams at the MTV Movie Awards and run up on stage with a passionate recreation of *The Notebook* kiss?" Now that I say it, it doesn't sound like a half bad idea.

"I think that might be just a little overboard, Jimmy." Lincoln wraps an arm around my shoulder and drops a kiss on my lips.

"Will you two stop making out already? I'm trying to get

drafted here." Janssen rolls his eyes from across the table, and Jamie chuckles next to him.

Those two are quite the pair, but she's managed to keep him in line and locked down for two years, so something must be going right.

We're all sitting at a table front and center in the large auditorium that the 2022 Professional Football Draft is being held in, since Lincoln and Janssen are among the top eligible players for teams to choose from. There is no doubt they'll both go in the first round, which is why they were given prime seating at a table surrounded by their friends and family. Have to give the cameras a good angle to watch us all ugly cry when their names get called.

To Lincoln's right are his parents, while Chase, Tyla, and Brant sit to my left. Janssen is flanked by his parents and one sister, who brought her husband with her. And then there is Jamie and me, the devoted girlfriends.

In the past two years, Lincoln and I have become more solid than ever. We've weathered college football seasons, his time away at the various training camps he's been invited to, a four-month stint where I studied in London with an internship at one of the top photography magazines in the world. We ate the long distance and swallowed it like champs. Because once we decided to be together, there was no other option.

He is my person, the one I can't wait to talk to about every little thing that happens in my day, and the man I can't fall asleep without. I help him through his vulnerable moments, especially the tough losses on the field, though there haven't been many. Last spring, he went on vacation with my parents and me, and they got to know him even better than they did from the couple of short visits we took home. They're officially obsessed with him, and I think my mom might want him for herself.

"Oh, here we go!" Lincoln's mom claps, shushing us, and we all turn to look at the commissioner who is walking out on to the stage.

"Welcome to the 2022 Professional Football Draft." He waits for the obligatory applause. "We have an exceptional class this year, and I know you men will go on to do great things both in and out of this league."

After a few more opening lines, he steps off stage. Now the clock is on for the first pick, the first team getting ten minutes to place their first-round pick.

"I can barely look." I hide my eyes in Lincoln's shoulder.

"No matter what happens, you're coming with me." He kisses my forehead.

We've already decided this. I have one year left of college, since Lincoln opted to leave early to declare for the draft, but after that, I'm moving to whichever city he gets signed by. I can always travel for work, or start my own local photography company. That's the blessing of my job, and I want to be where Lincoln is.

He's become the most important thing in my life, my career coming in a close second. It's funny, I always thought it would be the other way around, but I guess that's what happens when you're truly in love with someone.

Catherine goes through my mind almost daily, still. She'll be a person I never forget, and I even let Lincoln visit her grave with me recently. I try to go every time I'm home, but it's usually a solitary act. Finally, I was able to move through some of the stages of grief. What remains is a dull sadness each time I initially think of her, but the immediate feeling that follows is one of fond, happy memories. I believe she'd be proud of me, proud of where I am.

Looking at the clock, it's only been three minutes since the ten-minute window started.

"This is agony," I whine to Lincoln.

Just as I say it, the chime sounds over the auditorium, the whole crowd going into a whispered roar as we await the pick. Some guy in a suit walks on stage, holding an envelope. My heart begins beating so fast, I feel like I might pass out. Lincoln's hand that's laced through mine squeezes so hard, I just know he's on the edge of his seat.

"With the first pick in the draft, New York selects ... Lincoln Kolb!" he says.

Our whole table erupts into yelps, hugs and tears. I kiss Lincoln with everything I have as he stands, a goofy smile on his face, and buttons his suit jacket. Then he walks to the podium to take his rightful place as football's future legend.

I'm hugging his parents, Jamie, Janssen, everyone, when I hear his deep, charming voice come across the speaker system.

"I'd like to ask my girlfriend to come up here."

Lincoln is saying the words, but they don't fully sink in because I'm just in awe of this moment. It's like when you see people on TV, not able to react to things in real time because they're too caught up in the moment. I think I might black out, because when Chase is yelling at me to go up there, I'm thoroughly confused. But I stand, because Lincoln is motioning for me to join him.

My feet barely register that I'm walking up to the podium, the claps of those around me muted to my own ears. I feel like I'm in a tunnel, my vision only on Lincoln.

When I reach the stage, he takes my hand, helps me up the stairs. I give him a puzzled look, because I truly have no idea if me being up here is even allowed.

"I know this is a little unconventional," he says into the microphone, holding my hand with his free one. "But I told myself if I went first, I'd do this. There is no one else I'd rather share this moment with. You deserve every bit as much credit for getting us here as I do, and for as long as I'm blessed to play in this league, there is no one else I want by my side for the ride. So ..."

He places the microphone on the stand next to us and pulls something out of his jacket pocket.

And then kneels.

Holy. Shit.

"Oh my God." It pops out of my mouth because I can't think anything else.

"Henley, will you marry me?" Lincoln's face is shining so brightly, his smile warm and loving, portraying everything good and wonderful in this world.

What in the world? He opens the box he's holding up, and inside is a vintage gold band with a big center opal and a dozen tiny diamonds surrounding it. It looks like a flower and is so unique from what anyone else is wearing. He knows me so well that he can even pick out the perfect engagement ring without even asking my opinion.

Engagement ring. Marry him. The phrases race through my mind, and I swallow against the knot in my throat to get the words out.

"Of course. Yes!" I cry, lunging for him.

He catches me as he stands, and the cheers around us are deafening. I'm going to marry Lincoln Kolb. He's going to be my husband.

"You're stuck with me now, Jimmy," he whispers in my ear.

"Wouldn't want it any other way, Stallion," I breathe back.

As he slides the ring onto my finger, and we're ushered off the stage because holy moly have we eaten up a lot of broadcast time, I'm still in disbelief.

I might have started this whole thing as an elaborate trap, a way to fool Lincoln Kolb into falling in love with me.

In the end, though, the jokes on me. Not only did he fool me once, or twice, but he fools me endlessly. Though now, both of our eyes are open. We're clearly choosing to walk down this path together.

Lincoln is so clearly the mate my soul had been searching for that it was impossible not to fall into the trap of *him*.

I'd do it again, a thousand times over. Now I get to, every day, for the rest of my life.

Do you want your **FREE** Carrie Aarons eBook?

All you have to do is **<u>sign up for my newsletter</u>**, and you'll immediately receive your free book!

ALSO BY CARRIE AARONS

Standalones:

Love at First Fight

Nerdy Little Secret

That's the Way I Loved You

Fool Me Twice

Hometown Heartless

The Tenth Girl

You're the One I Don't Want

Privileged

Elite

Red Card

Down We'll Come, Baby

As Long As You Hate Me

All the Frogs in Manhattan

Save the Date

Melt

When Stars Burn Out

Ghost in His Eyes

On Thin Ice

Kissed by Reality

The Callahan Family Series:

Warning Track

ABOUT THE AUTHOR

Author of romance novels such as The Tenth Girl and Privileged, Carrie Aarons writes books that are just as swoon-worthy
as they are sarcastic. A former journalist, she prefers the love
stories of her imagination, and the athleisure dress code, much
better.

When she isn't writing, Carrie is busy binging reality TV,
having a love/hate relationship with cardio, and trying not to
burn dinner. She's a Jersey girl living in Texas with her husband,
daughter, son and Great Dane/Lab rescue.

Please join her readers group, Carrie's Charmers, to get the latest
on new books, as well as talk about reality TV, wine and home
decor.

You can also find Carrie at these places:
Website
Facebook
Instagram
Twitter
Amazon
Goodreads

Printed in Great Britain
by Amazon